THE REMOVAL COMPANY

Watch for the Next Appearance of Joe Scintilla:

Conspiracy of Silence; and, Tragedy at Sarsfield Manor
(A Wildside Double)—forthcoming 2011

THE REMOVAL COMPANY

A JOE SCINTILLA
HISTORICAL MYSTERY NOVEL

by

S. T. Joshi

THE BORGO PRESS

An Imprint of Wildside Press LLC

MMX

CONTENTS

CHAPTER ONE

"...This is pre-eminently the time to speak the truth, the whole truth, frankly and boldly. Nor need we shrink from honestly facing conditions in our country today. This great nation will endure as it has endured, will revive and will prosper. So first of all let me assert my firm belief that the only thing we have to fear is fear itself—nameless, unreasoning, unjustified terror which paralyzes needed efforts to convert retreat into advance...."

I was listening, in rapt attention, to that booming, faintly nasal voice on the radio—the voice that in the last year or so had become so familiar, the voice of Franklin Delano Roosevelt. And now, after what seemed an eternity after his election, it was now official. I glanced quickly at the calendar on my desk: March 4, 1933. The inauguration of FDR as our thirty-second president was finally taking place, and Let 'em Starve Hoover and his ineffectual minions were out on their ears. Their shameful treatment of the Bonus Army last summer still left a bad taste in everyone's mouth, but now you could feel the sense of relief, even of optimism, that here at last was a man who might actually do something about the Depression.

There was a knock on the door—shy, hesitant, and fearful, as they all are. I did not welcome the interruption.

"Come in," I almost barked.

The door opened. I was looking up at a tall, stocky man, extremely—almost excessively—well dressed in top coat and silk hat. A young-old face—young in years, but old in the haggard circles under the eyes. He was carrying a briefcase.

"Mr. Scintilla?" he asked timidly.

"Yeah."

He looked quickly behind him at the empty lobby.

"You...er, your receptionist isn't there."

I looked up at his eyes, coldly. "She isn't there because I don't have one. Not any more." The Depression had hit private detectives as hard as it had hit others.

He shambled into the room, almost sliding into the chair in front of my desk.

"You come highly recommended...."

I thought he was going to say more. When he didn't, I said: "Glad to hear it."

I guess I wasn't being very helpful, but I really did want to listen to that inauguration speech. I also didn't feel much like working today.

But my customer was not to be deterred. Gaining courage, he opened his briefcase with a crisp snap and proceeded to lay a succession of articles on my nearly empty desk:

A small business card, well printed, with only three words and a telephone number on it.

A photograph of a young woman.

A newspaper clipping—evidently a marriage announcement.

A notebook or diary—much written in.

After he had finished his work, he looked expectantly at me, as if he thought I could divine his purpose and intent from the mere act of laying objects on my desk. I looked blandly back at him, saying: "Yes?"

He picked up the business card and handed it to me. "Does that mean anything to you?"

I took it. This is what it read:

THE REMOVAL COMPANY
MUrray Hill 4-3802

I put it down. "No."

"It must be near here, don't you think?"—eagerly.

I looked down at the number again. "I guess so. This is obviously a Murray Hill phone number, and that sure is where we are now. What do you want me to do—call it?"

His eyes opened wide. "Good God, no!" The prospect actually appeared to horrify him. "I mean...not yet. Perhaps you will want to later...."

I was getting tired of this.

"Mister, maybe you'd better explain just what you want. Your name would be a good start."

He looked abashed. "Sorry...it's just—I mean.... The whole thing is so strange." He took a deep breath and expelled it. "My name is Arthur Vance. I'm from Los Angeles, but I'm currently staying with my uncle at 144 East 62nd Street. Maybe you've heard of my father, Henry Vance...."

"The Steamship King?"

He winced quickly. "You can call him that if you want. But he's a good man. He treats his people fairly...."

That may be, but everyone knew how he had gained control of the Pacific Mail Steamship Company after Collis P. Huntington's death in 1900. You had to admire his fancy footwork in snatching up that huge operation. Assuming you find rapacity of that sort admirable.

"We're not here to talk about your father," I said. "What is it that you want me to do?"

Vance ran well-manicured hands through his well-barbered hair. "You see, it's like this...." He picked up the notebook, then put it back down again. "No, that can come later," he said, more to himself than to me. Then he picked up the photograph:

"That's my wife, Katharine."

I took the picture. It had probably been done with an old Brownie, but the young woman in it was stylishly dressed and well posed. The snap had clearly been taken by a professional. The woman herself seemed a bit on the morose side, but lovely in flowing blonde hair and a white gown of what seemed to be taffeta.

"Very nice," I said, handing the photo back to Vance.

"That was taken five years ago, a month before we were married."

He put the photo back down on the desk, then picked up the newspaper clipping and handed it to me.

"Please read it," he said.

I read it:

MISS CAVALIERI TO WED

Miss Elena Cavalieri, of Cattolica, Italy, will be married on Wednesday, October 26, at 5 o'clock, at the Church of the Transfiguration to Mr. Harry Greenway, son of Mr. and Mrs. Stanford Greenway of 25 West Tenth Street. The ceremony will be performed by the Rev. Dr. Charles X. Feeney.

Miss Margaret Chandler of New Haven, Conn., will be the bridesmaid, and Mr. William Samford, of this city, will be the best man. The ceremony will be followed by a dinner at the Plaza given by the groom's parents.

Mr. Greenway and his bride will make their home in New York.

I put it back down. "Okay, what about it?"

He looked right in my eyes, wetting his lips before he said: "That woman is also my wife. It's her—it's Katharine." He seemed to be defying me to disbelieve him.

I picked up the clipping and looked at it again. There was a kind of resemblance, but not so strong as to be noticeable at first glance. "Are you sure?" I said.

"Oh, I know, the hair style is different, and maybe even the expression of the face. But it's her, I tell you! It is!"

Vance was getting agitated.

"All right, all right, it's her," I said. "What happened? Did you divorce her?"

"No." Vance's mouth worked some more. "That clipping was sent to me by—well, that doesn't matter.... Anyway, it's from the New York *Herald-Tribune* about six months ago.... You can see the date in the corner—October 21, 1932."

I saw it. "So what?"

Vance took another deep breath. "My wife committed suicide on September 15, 1931."

CHAPTER TWO

I don't know how most people become private detectives; maybe from the police force, maybe because they can't think of anything else to do. I came to it from a different direction.

Imagine Joe Scintilla a college boy!—Johns Hopkins U., no less. I was just a bit too young for the initial draft registration of May 1917, and by the time I did register a few months later I was already neck deep in books. I browsed into everything—English, history, philosophy, science—specializing in nothing. But when I finished, I had no desire to be a cog in someone else's machine: I had to strike out on my own.

But why a detective? Who can say at this point? Maybe I saw an ad in the back of a pulp magazine—*Black Mask*, probably. But even here there were some obstacles: the Pinkertons were out of the question—I detested their readiness to be strikebreaking thugs in the hands of capitalists; and both the Baltimore and the New York offices of the Continental Detective Agency had no openings at the time.

Maybe a detective is someone who needs to know a little bit about everything, but not a lot about anything. Sure, there are some technical matters—the new science of finger-printing, the art of wearing or placing a wire—but anyone can master these. The science of detection is the science of humanity: you have to be part psychologist, part researcher, part snoop. The *Black Mask* boys emphasize the gunplay, but that's a myth: in my twelve years on the job I haven't fired my gun more than twice in any given year.

I also quickly learned that the private detective's best weapon is his victim, his prey. My pal Henry Mencken told us often enough at meetings of the Saturday Night Club that no one ever came to grief by underestimating the stupidity of the average human being, and that rule has worked pretty well for me.

In the dozen years I'd been at this game I had had my share of tedium—couldn't remember how many spouses had wanted me to track down husbands or wives engaged in shenanigans of all kinds, but mostly of the sexual sort—but it always satisfied me when my quarry committed that fatal act of stupidity that sunk them. It was all pretty easy. It isn't that I'm so bright myself: I don't know everything, but I know where to find out what I didn't know. That's important.

There was one instance where a wife had actually blown her husband's brains out after I had told her of the mistress he had stashed in a studio apartment in Chelsea. What was that to me? I had done my job, been paid for my services, and that was the end of it. Did the guy have it coming? Maybe yes, maybe no. The woman herself would have plenty of time to reflect on her own folly behind bars. It sure is fortunate for most people that stupidity isn't a capital offense.

But if most of the cases I'd worked on were mundane, the matter that Arthur Vance had brought me was quite otherwise.

"I know it sounds crazy," he was saying, "but this whole business is crazy! That's my wife! It is!"—shaking the newspaper clipping in front of my face as if that would convince me.

It was obvious I was in the presence of a man not quite in control of his emotions, perhaps of his sanity. I wasn't afraid of this thin, wiry fop, but I didn't want to go through the bother of using physical force on him. Better to calm him down.

"Okay, Mr. Vance, it's your wife. It does look like her.... Now how do you explain how she can marry someone after she's dead?"

Vance suddenly got up from the chair and began pacing around the small office, his angular body moving jerkily, like a mechanism not properly oiled. "I don't know, but it's that...that Removal Company! I *knew* there was something strange with that operation...." Then, almost to himself: "What could he have done to her...?"

"Do you want to tell me the story?"

"All right." He sat down heavily. "It's a long story. A real long story." When there was no change in my bland expression: "You needn't worry about a fee. I'll pay you well."

Without warning he reached into the inside pocket of his suit jacket and slapped down a neatly tied wad of bills on my desk.

My first thought was that Vance was lucky to have been able to withdraw so large a wad of cash from a bank: FDR had declared a week-long national bank holiday beginning to-morrow, to prevent skittish depositors from taking out all their money and stuffing it in their mattresses. This thick stack of bills in front of me had clearly never been soiled by human hands.

"Ten thousand dollars," he said. "And that's just for starters. You may need more."

I looked down at the money, then looked up at him. My expression was—I hope—still bland.

"Mr. Vance, you haven't told me what it is you want me to do. Or are you paying me just to sit and listen?"

He took that as a little joke, and cracked a smile from one side of his mouth. He almost looked human at that point. "Well, believe it or not, listening is a big part of it. I've never told this to anybody, and just getting it off my chest will be something."

I reached in my drawer and handed him something I should have offered long before—a smoke.

To my surprise, he waved his hand impatiently. "No, I don't smoke." Neither did I. Another point in his favor. Filthy habit, smoking. I put the cigarettes back in the drawer.

"Okay, here's how it is," he began. He took a deep breath, as if about to plunge into some deep water for a long time, then said:

"Katharine and I were married in 1930—January 17. It was kind of an arranged marriage, you might say, although we really did love each other...or so I thought. Our families had known each other for years—we both live in San Marino, California—and I'd been friends with her since she was a teenager. You know," he said with a kind of rueful smirk, "it's funny about the wealthy. Everybody thinks you can do whatever you like, but you can't. I couldn't think of marrying outside of my social circle—it would have been unimaginable. And as for Katharine—well, she was in an even more difficult bind.

"You see, her father, Franklin Hawley, had been ruined in the stock market crash, and actually killed himself not long after. He was so ashamed—he knew that he would no longer be able to support his family in their accustomed style. Of course, they couldn't collect any life insurance. They were really in a bad way, although they tried to put the best face on it. Had to let go all their servants except their butler...."

"Must have been tough," I couldn't help interjecting.

Vance flushed beet-red. "I know what you're thinking: *Idle rich! Only one butler left to run the estate!* Well, it wasn't like that—it wasn't—"

"Okay, okay," I said. "I'm sorry. Please go on."

Vance glared at me a bit, but then softened. One more sweep of the hand through the hair.

"Frankly, Katharine's mother had to secure an advantageous marriage for her—it was the only thing to do. I guess she saw me as a good choice. And you know, we really were very fond of each other—did a lot of things together, always had a good time.... It made sense. So we started seeing a lot of each other, just to make sure we were really compatible—and we were. We really were."

Vance began to choke up a bit. Taking out a silk handkerchief, he mopped his brow, then rubbed his eyes a little.

"It started off fine. She came to live with us, of course—my parents and me—and we made sure that her mother had enough to live comfortably. Everything seemed to be working. We led a quiet life—neither of us liked parties very much—and we were talking about starting a family in a year or two.

"But Katharine had always been a bit glum—ever since I knew her as a kid. God knows why that was; maybe you'll find out a bit more from this"—he tapped the notebook he had placed on my desk—"but I guess no one will really ever know."

"Probably not," I said, just to say something. Vance had paused, not sure how to proceed.

"Well, I tried everything to make her happy. We traveled, I gave her whatever she wanted, I even offered to have her mother come and live with us. She was always close to her mother, especially after her father...." His mouth worked, as if some ill-tasting substance had fallen on his tongue. "She'd been seeing one of those psychoanalysts—a man who specialized in depression—and that seemed to cheer her up a little, but only for a while. Only for a while...."

He trailed off. I could tell what was coming—or so I thought. "And so she...?"

Vance, who had been looking down at my desk rather than at me, sprang to attention as if he had been slapped. "No! Not like that! It wasn't what you think!" His face contorted, in a mixture of pain, remorse, and bewilderment. "There's more to it than that...."

And this is what he said.

CHAPTER THREE

"Arthur, please sit down here for a moment." Katharine patted the space on the couch next to her.

I knew what she was going to say before she said it; and yet, it was still a jolt—still something so incomprehensible that I could hardly believe my ears, hardly believe it was not a bad dream from which I'd awake if I tried hard enough.

"I think...."—even she was having trouble saying it, although she had surely been thinking it for a long time—"I think I want to die."

If I had been less stunned by her words, I should have suspected something odd about the way she chose to make that statement. She didn't say: "I want to kill myself"; she said, "I want to die."

What can you say when someone says a thing like that?—especially someone who is your wife, someone scarcely more than twenty-six years old, someone you thought you loved and who you thought loved you? I could not speak; but I felt beads of perspiration sprouting on my forehead, and I began shaking all over. Finally:

"Katharine, darling, you can't mean that...."

I'm sure she had been preparing for a reaction like that, for she started speaking almost immediately, like a schoolgirl giving a rehearsed speech.

"Oh, Arthur, I know what you must be thinking.... But please don't think it has anything to do with you! I love you dearly, but it's something I really have to do. It's my only way of taking control of my life, don't you see?"

She looked at me almost pleadingly. Then, unable to suppress her nervous energy, she almost leaped up from the couch and began pacing about.

"I've been thinking about this for a long time. It's the only way! Oh, Arthur!"—as if she were exasperated by my stupidity—"I'm so useless! I have nothing to live for! I don't serve any purpose!"

I was stung. "You can live for me. I love you."

I said it with a calmness that even now strikes me as eerie. Perhaps I was already becoming resigned to the inevitable.

Katharine seemed a bit taken aback; maybe she was expecting me to scream, shout, throw a tantrum. She sat down beside me again and put both her hands on my cheeks:

"Arthur, dearest, a person can't live for someone else. Can't you see that? I have to have my *own* reasons for living! I've done nothing in my life, and don't see how I ever will. There's so much waste in the world, Arthur...."

By now I was getting angry. I was hurt, but more than that, I was deeply insulted. Katharine was making *me* feel worthless. I shouldn't have said it, but I did:

"Katharine, if it's because of what your father did...."

It was a mistake. Leaping up from the couch, she turned on me with a rage I had never seen in her before:

"Don't you *dare* bring up my father! He was a far better man than you'll ever know. What he did was the bravest, most decent..." She became speechless with fury.

"I'm sorry, Katharine...." I went to her, tried to comfort her by putting my arms around her shoulders, but she shook me off. She'd never done that before. Then she tried to get a grip on herself, taking some deep breaths and looking fixedly at the floor.

"I told you I've been thinking about this for a long time. I don't think there's been a day in the last ten years when I *haven't* thought about it." That means she had been thinking about this since she was about fifteen. "Do you take me for some flighty, irrational creature who's come to this decision on a whim? I thought you'd give me more credit than that, Arthur! Can't you see this is my *life* we're talking about?" Her eyes glared at me like a Gorgon's.

I thought I'd better take a different tack. I knew that she'd spent much of her life in a depression, and that a lot of people had hovered around her in a futile attempt to make her happy and normal. Probably they'd ended up just irritating her. Although I wouldn't in the least think of her as argumentative—that would have been so contrary to how she had been taught a lady should behave—I could see she had a kind of quiet, desperate determination that fueled itself upon opposition.

"All right, Katharine," I said in a soothing voice that I hoped had no trace of patronage or condescension, "let's say you want to do...what you want to do. How exactly do you intend to go about it?"

The response was anything but what I would have expected. Stunned as I was by this whole turn of events, I was even more stupefied by what she now did.

For she changed her demeanor entirely and became eager, dynamic, even cheerful in an appalling way. She flung herself around, went to her handbag lying on the bureau, and fished around inside. She then drew out a business card and silently handed it to me, with a weird gesture of triumph. It read:

THE REMOVAL COMPANY
MUrray Hill 4-3802

I could hardly utter for a moment. Then: "What's this?"

"Dr. Grabhorn told me about it," she said with that hideous eagerness that was chilling me more and more. "He didn't really explain what they do, but I think they must...you know, *help* people who...."

It was now my turn to dance with rage.

"*Grabhorn!* I knew it! That wretch! I knew that witch-doctor was behind all this! If I ever—"

Katharine interrupted me with the simple gesture of holding her hand calmly in front of her.

"Arthur, you don't understand. Dr. Grabhorn has been *wonderful* to me. He's helped me so much! If it weren't for him, I would have done this a long time ago. But even he can't help me now—not that way. But he can help me *this* way."

Grabhorn was one of those psycho-analysts—disciple of Freud, evidently; had even met the eminent Austrian on a trip to Europe years ago. Katharine had been going to see him for the better part of two years. He apparently had a very exclusive clientele—only the best (that is, the richest) for him. He didn't come cheap.

I was rapidly losing control of the entire situation, and also of my emotions. My head was spinning. It was too much to digest—and even if I could digest it, the whole thing was so repulsive that my mind refused to accept even the least part of it.

"Wait a minute, Katharine.... What exactly does this 'Removal Company' do? You don't mean to tell me that they...that they *kill* people?"

She took on a peculiar expression—rather sheepish, as if apologizing for some *faux pas*. "Well, yes, I guess they do. Dr. Grabhorn doesn't even know the details himself, and of course it's all very secret and confidential.... I mean, we'd have to go to New York—that's where the place is—and I think we'd have to sign some papers, and apparently it's pretty expensive...they're taking on an awfully big risk, you know."

This was sounding awfully fishy. "Katharine, there's something funny about all this...."

"Oh, Arthur, there isn't!" Again that eagerness, mixed now with impatience. "Dr. Grabhorn wouldn't get me into anything unsavory! He's such a dear, dear man. But don't you see, it has to be a secret.... My God, Arthur, the whole thing's illegal, you know—at least illegal according to the laws we have...maybe someday it will be different. But there are so many people who need help in this way...so many! I think it's wonderful that there's someone who has the courage to do something like this. But I guess the ordinary person would think of it as *murder*...." She looked pensively off in the distance, with the look of someone pondering an abstract problem in philosophy.

My whole body was beginning to shake uncontrollably. I couldn't believe I was talking about this—talking about having someone kill my wife because she wanted to die and apparently couldn't bring herself to do it alone. I had to sit on the couch. I really needed a drink, but I didn't want to leave Katharine alone at a time like this. There had to be a way to persuade her out of this crazy plan.

"Katharine, have you called these people yet?" I could tell at a glance that it was a New York telephone number, even though no address was given.

"Well, no," she said, shyly. "I thought you might want to...."

"Me!" I thundered.

"Oh, Arthur, please help me! I can't do this by myself. I need your help!"

In every other situation except this one, I would have rushed to her aid—would have done so without her even having to ask. But this was too much.

"Katharine, I won't do it...."

"Arthur!" She broke down crying, throwing herself on her bed.

I felt as if some demon were twisting my insides into knots. I think for a moment that I wanted to die myself.

What was I to do? How far would I have to go to bring her back from the precipice? Would I fall over the precipice myself? What would be the outcome? Could it be anything, now, but a tragedy?

I resigned myself to the inevitable—at least for now. I wasn't giving up; let's just say I was performing a tactical retreat. I would save Katharine, but now was not the time to challenge her.

"All right, dearest," I said, coming over to her and stroking her hair. "I'll call them. I'll call the Removal Company."

CHAPTER FOUR

We were on the train heading for New York.

The whole adventure had taken on a dreamlike quality: Loading our baggage (Katharine's a lot smaller than mine, since—in her view, at any rate—she would only require clothes and accessories for a one-way trip) into our Aston Martin saloon...being driven to the Passenger Rail Terminal on Alameda Street...settling into our private Pullman car...shoving off for the five-day trip—Los Angeles to New York, via New Orleans and Washington, D.C....

It was the most harrowing and bizarre five days of my life—even more bizarre, I think, than what followed. What made it so was Katharine's attitude of grotesque *cheerfulness*. She was as effervescent as a schoolgirl, constantly pointing out novel bits of scenery through the window, taking a childish delight in the meals we ate (we had our own private dining car, of course: fraternizing with the other passengers was, under the circumstances, unthinkable, even though they were mostly of our class), and, in essence, enjoying life as I'd never seen her enjoy it before.

Knowing that the burden of existence was soon to be sloughed off had, it seemed, liberated her in some strange way: the simplest, most mundane aspects of life gained that much more sweetness because she knew that she would soon be rid of them. For a few fleeting moments I thought that maybe she was making the right decision after all....

No! I wouldn't let myself think that! What she was contemplating was appalling, immoral—and, fundamentally, selfish. What right does anyone have willfully and deliberately to truncate the life-span they have been given? How could one be so self-absorbed, so heedless of others' feelings? And yet, the doubts would come.... Was *I* being self-ish? Did I want her to live just to suit my own pleasure, my own needs? And why was it that my own love for her seemed to matter so little in her decision? How could I not feel scorned, humiliated, in-sulted?

You can imagine—or can you?—the turmoil of emotions I was undergoing. I could hardly eat, slept badly, and was driven almost out of my mind by watching Katharine so cheerful and lively! (No, that's a bad word to use....) I think she took pity on me after a while and tried to suppress her eagerness, her vibrancy, her positive *thrill* at the prospect of self-destruction...self-annihilation conveniently done by another party without trouble or inconvenience to herself.

Of course, I was still holding out the hope that she would recoil at the last minute. Neither Katharine nor I were under any silly religious delusions about the immortality of the soul or anything of that sort. We went to church, of course, but that was largely to please our parents and because it was a part of our social obligation. But we both knew full well that the only thing that follows death is complete oblivion.

And there, perhaps, was my last hope. Perhaps that very thought—*complete oblivion*—might pull her back at the final moment. Try to picture it, Mr. Scintilla: the utter elimination of the self, the total snuffing out of all consciousness. Far, far deeper than the most dreamless sleep, far more permanent than the longest epoch.... Nothingness. It was scarcely any wonder that most people refused to accept so horrible a fate and claimed to believe in that "better life" that they know in their heart of hearts will not come....

We had to change trains at New Orleans, and again at Washington. With each passing mile my apprehension grew, while Katharine was less and less able to conceal what now became an actual glee at the termination of her own existence. I began to measure every word I spoke to her, wondering how close it was to the last I would ever say to her.

At New York we checked into the Murray Hill Hotel at Park Avenue between 40th and 41st Streets. It was September 13, 1931. I didn't know it then, but my wife had two days to live.

* * * * * * *

The rest of the episode was in many ways an anticlimax—so mundane on the surface that I could scarcely keep in my mind that Katharine had come here to put an end to her life.

We had called shortly after we had settled into our room, and made an appointment with the Removal Company for the next day. Even now we were not given the address of the place: they had politely but firmly refused to do so when I had first phoned them in Los Angeles, and now all they said was that we were to meet a black Packard in front of the Waldorf at 2 P.M.

Sure enough, at exactly that hour a car answering the description pulled up at the kerb. I waved at it tentatively, and it drew up to us. The window was rolled down slowly on the passenger side of the front seat, and the driver—apparently a short, stocky man of middle age with a bullet head and what I can only describe as *dead* features, no vitality or expression in them at all—craned his neck out the window.

"Vance?" he said in his flat voice. It was barely a question.

I nodded.

He said nothing, but with a head gesture he indicated that we get in the back seat. It was clear he didn't want company with him in front.

After we had settled in—Katharine almost leaping in ahead of me, and then bouncing on the seat like a little girl—Bullet Head turned around and glared blankly at us.

"Put these on," he said, handing us black silk handkerchiefs.

I was nonplussed: did he want me to put the handkerchief in my suit pocket—around my hat—around my neck? What? As we both looked stupidly at him, he deigned to clarify, with not a little impatience:

"Over your eyes."

This was too ridiculous. I suddenly felt I was in a vaudeville act, or in a story from some cheap pulp magazine.

"You can't be serious—"

"Put—them—on."

His tone was so unexpectedly hostile that we backed away from him. At that, Bullet Head relented a bit.

"Please...." The word seemed not to come easily out of his mouth, for he grimaced momentarily as if in pain. "Doctor's orders. Just for... security. We need to protect ourselves."

We did as we were told. Katharine complied readily, still smiling broadly as though the whole episode were a game.

The point, of course, was to throw us off our bearings, to confuse us, to prevent us from knowing where we were going—and it worked. Bullet Head seemed to take far too many turns than was necessary to reach his destination, and in our blindfolded state we quickly became disoriented, even a bit queasy. I clutched Katharine's hand with a kind of desperation. Mine felt clammy, and I could feel hers tremble a bit. Possibly this grotesque charade was causing the reality of the whole thing to sink into her consciousness at last.

We finally pulled up to a kerb somewhere—traffic seemed surprisingly scanty, so I suspect we were on a side street. When we had come to a stop I instinctively began to take off the blindfold, but Bullet Head actually reached over the seat and grabbed my hand, squeezing it hard.

"*No*...not yet. Keep still."

I relaxed my hand, so that he could tell I was prepared to follow his orders.

I heard him get out of the car, slam the door, and then walk around the car to my side. Opening the door, he took my arm, firmly but not roughly, and drew me out. I stumbled a bit—we were not as close to the kerb as I had thought—but managed to reach what I took to be the sidewalk. Bullet Head let go of me and apparently helped Katharine out of the car. I could hear her utter a faint moan—not, apparently, from anything Bullet Head was doing, but possibly from confusion or nerves.

Evidently the man was now between us, and he took each of our arms and led us forward. We walked a considerable distance—far too long a distance if we were merely entering some building in front of the sidewalk—so I guessed that we were actually in some alley. It was very silent, only the crunching of our shoes on rough pavement reaching my ears. Strangely enough, I wasn't afraid: I felt completely passive, and scarcely worried or cared whether I myself would come out of this escapade alive or not.

After what seemed an eternity Bullet Head tugged our arms as an indication that we should stop. Some keys rattled in his pocket, one key was fitted into a door, then another, and then the door opened. A faint trace of a strange odor—chemicals of some sort—tickled our nostrils. Bullet Head motioned us forward, but stopped us almost immediately with the single word: "Stairs."

The stairs were of concrete, apparently. There were about twenty of them, constituting a single flight. At the top we were again asked to stop, while Bullet Head fished for more keys and opened another door. We entered, and, as the door closed behind us, we were finally permitted to take off our blindfolds.

I initially had difficulty understanding what I saw. The room seemed to be shaped in a perfect hexagon, and everything in it, except one object, appeared to be white: ceiling, floor, walls, even the desk and chair in the exact center of the room. The one thing that was not white looked at first like a head floating in mid-air—until I realized that it was connected to a man, dressed entirely in white, and standing in front of the desk.

The man seemed about forty or forty-five. He was tall, slim, his close-cropped hair quite gray. He was clean shaven, and had the most vivid green eyes I have ever seen. His face seemed unusually tanned and seamed, but otherwise there was only an expression of calm, placid intelligence on his countenance. He did not smile.

"Mr. and Mrs. Vance?" he said in a quiet, modulated voice. At our nod: "Welcome. I am Doctor Sanderson. You have come to the Removal Company."

CHAPTER FIVE

It was only when Dr. Sanderson gestured to them that I saw there were two chairs—also in white—directly behind him, in front of the desk. In a kind of daze Katharine and I sat down in them, Sanderson walking with measured pace to sit in the chair behind the desk. For several moments there was complete silence.

Then Dr. Sanderson made a tent of his fingers and said quietly:

"My dear sir and madam, I trust you realize why you are here."

Katharine suddenly leaned forward and began: "Yes, of course! Isn't it all arranged? When—"

She stopped abruptly when Sanderson held up a hand, gently. It seemed he was incapable of any movement that was not calm, quiet, and composed.

"One moment, Mrs. Vance. There are some...preliminaries."

He opened a drawer in the desk and drew out a clipboard. Then he continued:

"I really know very little about the two of you. I have only spoken once on the phone to Mr. Vance, and have not spoken to Mrs. Vance at all. We need to take care of some things first."

Katharine seemed upset—far more upset than at any time since leaving Los Angeles. "You're not going to try to talk me out of.... Oh! how could you, after we've come all this way!"

"Be assured," Sanderson said. "I have no desire to persuade you to do or not to do anything. Your wishes are your own; I am entirely at your service to fulfill them."

He got up and began to pace about, slowly.

"You realize, of course, that what we are about to do is, to be blunt, contrary to the laws of this nation? And you do realize that it is I who will absorb all the risks involved in this...operation? It is, indeed, quite possible that, if detected, I could receive the harshest penalty that our system of justice has in its arsenal...."

It was now my turn to be angry. "Sanderson, if you're worried about your money, I have it right here." I began to reach for the brief-case I had brought with me, but once again that hand of his restrained me. He wore a look of contempt on his face.

"I am not concerned about the money. I am aware that you have brought the money. Frankly, I would do this for no money, as a human service."

He sat down again at his desk.

"My concern, Mr. Vance"—he looked directly at me with a gaze that made me feel queerly humiliated—"is that you have no second thoughts about this procedure. Pardon me for saying so, but it is not possible for Mrs. Vance to have any second thoughts in the matter. But you..."

"I don't like what we're doing," I said harshly, heedless of what effect my words might have on Katharine, "but if it's what my wife wants, then that's all that matters."

"Very admirable of you." I couldn't tell if there was sarcasm in his voice. "But time has a way of affecting one's feelings. So I trust you will not object to signing this."

He wheeled the clipboard around and thrust it at me.

"What is this?" I said.

"Merely a statement that you have participated in this affair. By signing it you make yourself...I believe the legal term is *accessory*. In this case, an accessory before the fact. You should be aware that in some cases the punishment for that is as severe as for...." He did not need to complete the sentence.

For some reason I had not expected this. Apparently Katharine had, for she was not looking shocked or surprised in the least, but instead was merely sitting calmly with hands folded and eyes fixed on a blank spot on the desk in front of her.

I became agitated—almost leaped from my chair. "What...what will you do with that paper if I sign it?"

Dr. Sanderson looked up at me as if I were a foolish schoolboy. "Why, nothing, Mr. Vance...assuming that you say or do nothing in the future about this business. Surely you understand that if I were to implicate you, I would be implicating myself. Quite frankly, I would have preferred working with Mrs. Vance alone, but since you insisted on coming, I have to...protect myself."

"How do I know you won't keep extorting more money from me to keep quiet about this?" I said, hotly. "This sounds like a pretty neat scheme for perpetual blackmail."

Again those green eyes blazed at me, but now they seemed colder, filled with scorn and derision. But his tone of voice didn't waver—it remained uncannily calm and even gentle.

"If you do not wish to accept my word as a gentleman and a scientist that nothing of the sort will happen, you can perhaps take comfort in the fact that, if I may use a vulgar locution, we each have the other over a barrel. You could blackmail me just as easily as I could blackmail you."

I sat back down, grabbing the edge of the desk.

"Yes...yes, I see." I picked up the clipboard, scanned the paper. It had very little writing on it.

Sanderson handed me a pen. I took it, signed two copies of the document, thrust one copy back at him, and stuffed the other in my coat pocket.

With a curt "Thank you" he put the sheet of paper back in his desk. Then he turned to Katharine:

"My dear Mrs. Vance, there is a similar form that I should like to have you sign." He edged the clipboard in her direction; there was another sheet of paper on it. "I fear that your consenting to this act is no legal defense for what our society considers to be the crime we are committing, but it may be of some minimal help in the event of...untoward developments."

"Yes, of course," she said, eagerly taking the pen and signing the document with hardly more than a glance at it. There was, clearly, no need for her to sign in duplicate.

"Very well." Sanderson got up. "I shall see you again tomorrow, at this same time." He turned to leave.

Katharine looked as if someone had slapped her face. "But...Dr. Sanderson! I thought...we would...."

Sanderson turned around slowly. "You thought it would be today? Why, no. I think you need a day to contemplate matters—perhaps to take care of any final details. One more day of life will not hurt you."

If his smile had been a fraction of an inch longer than it was, I would have thought he was indulging in some kind of fiendish mockery. As it was, it was difficult to think of him as meaning anything but what he said.

He left the room by a door opposite from the one we had entered. I felt a sense of utter emptiness, of unreality. I haven't any idea what Katharine was feeling: disappointment, frustration, regret, panic, confusion? All these things seemed registered on her face, none overmastering the others. All we could do was get up and look about in a daze.

Bullet Head was still in the room—he had been behind us, standing at attention, the entire time. Now he held out the two black silk blindfolds in each hand. He didn't need to speak; we put them on.

* * * * * * *

I can't even begin to describe to you what that last night was like. After her initial disappointment, Katharine regained her horrible cheerfulness, knowing that tomorrow would be the end she had longed for. Perhaps the reality of the thing was sinking into me, for I made little effort to dissuade her or even to talk about the matter. It seemed pointless. I still held out a hope that she would pull back at the last moment, but I think I knew in my heart that she wouldn't.

My only recollections of that evening are disconnected fragments: a Broadway show...Katharine pulling my arm to lead me into some shop full of stuffed animals...a ride on a horse-drawn carriage in Central Park, just as if we were ordinary tourists...steaming hot chocolate in a café somewhere, as the night was getting chilly...Katharine giddy with some appalling excitement...laughing gaily over nothing, whirling herself on the sidewalk like a top, tossing herself joyfully on the bed in our hotel room, finally overcome with exhaustion....

It was almost too much for me. All evening a kind of lead weight had been growing in my stomach, so that I could hardly eat, talk, or even look at her toward the end. It seemed so utterly futile to discuss the matter with her: her mind seemed so completely made up—I knew she wouldn't be so deucedly *happy* if it weren't. Anyway, it seemed a shame to spoil her evening by bringing up anything unpleasant.

Would she pull back at the last moment—the very moment when she knew her action was irrevocable, inevitable, and utterly final? It was all I could hope for.

In a whirl the morning passed—a lavish room-service breakfast, scarcely touched by me but attacked with relish by Katharine...a stroll in Madison Square Park, Katharine taking particular interest in a squirrel that approached her hesitantly and, with a sudden dart, snatched the acorn she held out smilingly...back to the hotel and a light luncheon, Katharine showing no sign that it was to be her last....

Bullet Head was on time, as I could have predicted. A repeat of the blindfolds, the circuitous drive, the tramp up concrete steps, and the stark white room again.

This time Dr. Sanderson led us without delay through a door at the back of the room and into a much larger space—an elegantly furnished room with dark wooden paneling on the walls, a thick shag carpet on the floor, and several doors, unmarked and leading who knows where. He steered us to one of the several couches in the room, and we sat—I dropping heavily on to it, Katharine barely able to restrain herself and sitting at the very edge. Sanderson sat on a couch facing us.

He did not waste time.

"Mrs. Sanderson, do you understand what we are about to do?"

I think the "we" confused her for a moment—perhaps she envisaged some kind of collective suicide. But she shook off her doubt.

"Yes, of course."

"You have no second thoughts?"

"None, doctor. Absolutely none."

"You are completely resolved in this action? You are at peace with your decision?"

"Yes!" There was more than a little impatience in her voice. Then a slight furrow on her brow.

"Well, there's only one thing.... You haven't told me—us"—a

quick, harried glance in my direction—"what exactly is involved in the...procedure. Exactly what will you do...?"

Sanderson held up a hand in his habitual gesture to enjoin silence, although in fact Katharine did not seem inclined to say anything more.

"It is better that you not know." He glanced at me also, suggesting that his comment applied to me as well. "Rest assured that there will be no pain. That is exactly why I am here. Believe me—no pain."

Katharine actually beamed. "Oh, I believe you, doctor! I do!"

It sounded like some unholy marriage vow.

Sanderson got up. "Very well," he said heavily. "I think it is time."

All of a sudden I felt horribly dizzy, as if I were teetering on the edge of a cliff. My last hope—that the finality of the thing would cause Katharine to recoil—was dashed. I was in a panic—I felt like shrieking, I wanted to grab Katharine, even against her will, and flee this loathsome place, to stamp on Sanderson's seamed, placid face until it was a mass of broken bones and flesh....

But all I did was to croak feebly, "Katharine...."

She held up a hand just as Sanderson had done.

"No, Arthur. It's too late. I have decided. This is what I want." Her expression was neither cheerful nor sad, neither excited nor calm. Instead, it was utterly blank. She could have been a corpse already.

She gave me a chaste kiss on the cheek. That was all.

Sanderson led her away through one of the doors—I hardly knew which one. Instinctively I reached for her, but Bullet Head—unobtrusively standing behind us, as always—suddenly came forward and grabbed my arm; not violently, but firmly.

I gave up. I knew it was hopeless now. I merely sat down on the couch, my face in my hands.

I have no idea how many minutes passed before I heard a door opening. It was Sanderson. His expression was as placid as ever; it was as if nothing had happened.

I looked up at him, a mute inquiry on my face.

He merely said: "It is over."

I didn't know what to do or say. Should I rave like a maniac or walk calmly out of the place? Should I throttle him, or shake his hand? I'm not sure that what I had actually done—what I had been a party to—had fully sunk into my consciousness. The room began to spin again, and the doctor in his white suit looked like some spectre bent on haunting me the rest of my days.

"What...what did you do?" I said weakly.

He merely looked at me with a mildly irritated expression, but said nothing. I had forgotten: it was better that I not know.

"Do you think...I can see her?" I stammered.

His eyes flickered for a moment. "I do not think that is wise."

I almost leaped from the couch. "But I have to see her! Just one last time! Surely that's not too much to ask...."

Sanderson seemed a bit agitated, even alarmed, at my outburst. That hand went up again.

"Very well, Mr. Vance. But I warn you that such an experience is usually very painful to the...survivors. Please take care."

I nodded dumbly, and followed him through a door. There, on what appeared to be a wheeled hospital bed—the only object of furniture in the small room—was Katharine. A sheet covered everything but her face.

I went over to her. I wondered whether I should touch her—whether Sanderson would chide me, or even physically prevent me from so doing, or whether I could endure the horror of it. I gently reached out and brushed her cheek with my fingers. It was already cold.

With a strangled cry I wheeled around, no longer able to stand any of this—my dead wife, the placid Sanderson, the antiseptic surroundings, the bullet-headed factotum.... Then I turned back, gazed for what seemed to be minutes at Katharine's face, hoping against hope to see some faint trace of animation—the flicker of an eyelid, the rise and fall of her chest, the return of color to her cheeks...but there was nothing.

Very quietly, very gently, I bent down and pressed my warm lips against her cold ones. They yielded, softly, as dough yields when pressed by a thumb. There was no response.

CHAPTER SIX

By this time Vance and I were almost finished with a meal at Delmonico's. Evidently his lofty social status was a sufficient cover for my lack of proper evening dress. I'll admit this was one of the better meals I've had lately. Vance didn't eat much—was too busy talking—but I didn't follow his example, either in the eating or in the talking.

He was scowling down at his dessert and coffee, as if one or the other contained some blemish that offended his sense of decorum. I saw no problem with what was in front of me. But when Vance continued silent, I felt I had to say something.

"If you want to rest a while and take up your story later…."

"No!" It could have been Bullet Head speaking. "No...just let me think a bit. I want to finish."

For once I wished one of my clients actually did smoke—it might calm him. Instead, he shot a hand through his hair, swallowed a large mouthful of scalding coffee without apparently tasting it, and went on:

"You can't imagine what sort of complications this whole business created. First of all, of course, there was the matter of what to do with... with the...."

"The body?" I supplied.

Vance glared at me. "Yes," he said heavily, turning away from me. "Although I should have known that Sanderson had that all taken care of. When I asked him, all he said was, 'I will deal with it,' in that bland, toneless voice of his. I suppose he must have had some means...." The memory of it caused Vance's face to writhe in pain. "God, I can't even bear to think of it! Heaven only knows what he did....

"Anyway, that was by no means the end of it. Naturally, we hadn't told our families what we were doing—and the explanations were... well, shall we say, they weren't very convincing. It would positively have killed Katharine's mother if she ever found out—a husband already dead by suicide, and now a daughter.... No, it would have been too much. She herself might have...."

Vance swallowed hard, put the thought out of his mind, and proceeded.

"All I said, when I got back to San Marino, was that Katharine and I had had a big fight and she had left me—gone off on her own. I also had to say that she felt some deep resentment against my family, and that's why we shouldn't expect her to write to any of us.... In a way that wasn't much of a lie: I wouldn't say she resented my family's wealth and standing so much as that she was constantly having to face the fact that we still *had* wealth and standing whereas her own family didn't. I think it made her feel rather like chattel when she married me.... Well, that's of no importance now.

"How to explain why she didn't write to her own mother was the difficulty. She had been very close to her father, and took his death hard, but she also loved her mother deeply; and it wounded Mrs. Hawley terribly that she wasn't receiving any messages from her daughter. In fact, she spent quite a bit of money hiring some private eye here in New York to look for Katharine, but of course he found nothing—not the faintest trace of a lead."

"Do you mind my asking," I said, "how much Sanderson charged for his...services?"

Vance looked blankly at me and said: "One hundred thousand dollars."

My coughing fit lasted for several minutes.

"I know what you're going to say," Vance continued after he was sure I had regained control of myself. "I was a sucker. But he was right about one thing: he really was taking a big risk doing what he was doing...assuming he actually *did* do it.... I mean, what he did was *murder*, isn't it? Helping a person commit suicide is murder, right?"

"Yes," I said. "Legally, anyway."

"What do you mean by that?" Vance said sharply.

"Nothing.... I only meant that the law regards it as murder, and Sanderson could conceivably be sent to the chair. My own views on the matter aren't important."

Vance continued to peer at me, as though he might ferret out some nugget of information from my face, but finally gave it up.

"Anyway, that's what I gave him. That was the deal. And he made me sign that paper so that I wouldn't go to the police—because then he could involve me in the matter." Vance took another swig of coffee. It wasn't hot any more.

I scratched my head. "Mr. Vance, your story is very peculiar, and very touching also." I meant that honestly—wasn't being snide. "But what exactly do you want me to do? You sounded pretty sure, when you saw your wife lying there on that bed in Sanderson's office, or whatever it was, that she was...well, that she was dead."

"I know that." Vance looked around the room, for no apparent reason. "But maybe it was a trick! I'm sure now that it was a trick!"

"Why?"

That brought him up short. "What do you mean, why?"

"Why do you think it was a trick?"—patiently.

"Because of this!" And he brought out his clipping from the *Herald-Tribune*.

I glanced at it, then looked back at him. "You think this...this Elena Cavalieri...is your wife." It was a statement, not a question.

"*I* don't think so! I mean, I *do*, but I'm not the only one! Don't you see?" He was almost enraged with frustration: by the way he was looking at me, I must have been the world's prize moron. "This was sent to me by my friend, Gene Merriwether. He works on the *Herald-Tribune*. We go back a long way...our families know each other, and he and I went to Berkeley together...in fact, he must have met Katharine then also, although she was a freshman and we were seniors.... Anyway, he came east to pursue a career in journalism, but so far he's been stuck doing the society columns. Since he's California blue-blood, I guess his paper thinks he knows something about the Four Hundred...."

Vance seemed irritated, reflecting again on the world's varied injustices to blue-bloods, then went on: "He was doing some background work on an article on the Greenways, and he came upon this six-month-old clipping in the paper's 'morgue.' It was he who sent it to me. He himself said it was Katharine!"

I looked at Vance skeptically. "Merriwether said this was your wife?"

Vance backed off. "Well, not in so many words.... But he sent it to me because he felt there was a striking resemblance!"

"Okay, let's say for the sake of argument that this Elena woman does look like your wife. What of it? What are you saying or suggesting?"

"I don't know exactly," Vance said, now a bit tentative. "But there's something funny going on—something very funny indeed...."

"Vance, I'll go even farther. Let's say this actually *is* your wife. What do you think happened?—that Sanderson brought her back from the dead, and that he then gave her some entirely new personality? Look at the clipping, Vance: *Elena Cavalieri, of Cattolica, Italy.* Whoever wrote this article—I presume it wasn't Merriwether himself—must have been supplied this information. What reason do you have, aside from some supposed resemblance to your wife, that this woman isn't who it says she is?"

Vance said nothing.

"How about this?" I suggested. "You say this Gene Merriwether knew your wife, although apparently not well." I looked up at him to confirm this assumption; when Vance made no remark, I felt I was on safe ground. "Then how well does he know Elena Cavalieri? Did he cover this wedding?"

"No," Vance said in a small voice.

"Has he ever seen or met Miss Cavalieri—now Mrs. Greenway?"

"I don't think so."—even smaller.

"So," I concluded, with a sigh of impatience, "on the basis of a photograph in a newspaper clipping that someone who doesn't know your wife very well thinks looks like her, even though she supposedly died a year and a half ago, you've come to me to investigate this matter." It was again a statement, not a question.

Vance was looking down at his plate, with its untouched dessert. "Yes."

"I think you're wasting your time and your money."

He glanced up quickly, simultaneously alarmed and crestfallen. "Does that mean...that you won't do anything?"

Suddenly I felt an overwhelming pity for the fellow. He really was in a bad way. "Mr. Vance, I think you've gone through a horrible experience; I think you're tormented with guilt at what happened, even though I for one don't think you're in any way to blame in all this. And now you're grabbing at straws. Maybe you should just accept the fact that your wife is dead, and get on with your life."

Vance sat quiet for a few moments—then exploded with rage. "Who are you to tell me what to do, Scintilla? Don't you dare preach at me! Whose side are you on, anyway?" He had turned bright red and was breathing heavily and irregularly.

"I'm not on anybody's side," I said with all the calmness I could muster. "I don't know that there are any sides to be on. My feeling is that the matter doesn't warrant investigation. There's too little to go on. There are a variety of ways to look into it, and there's a lot I could do in terms of checking the backgrounds of all these people, but I very much doubt that the end result will be anything you want or hope for."

"But what about this Removal Company? Don't you think it's a fishy operation? And it's right here in your own back yard...." Vance now seemed more desperate than angry.

"I'm not the police. Even if I find this Sanderson fellow, I can't make any arrests. Anyway, if I did go to the police, that would get you into a bit of trouble, wouldn't it?"

"Yes, I suppose so." Vance rubbed his chin. "But please: could you just look around a bit? Do whatever you can—don't go to the police, but just report back to me if you come up with anything...peculiar. I just want to set my mind at ease." Vance leaned back heavily in his chair and closed his eyes.

I put my napkin down on the table and called for the check. "All right, Vance. But I'll tell you one thing: I'm not likely to use a fraction of that ten thousand dollars you plumped down on my desk. So I'll get to work, and take whatever fee I think appropriate for my time and expenses, and give back what's left. And I suspect a lot will be left. Okay?"

"Okay." Vance paid the check without looking at it.

"I may need your help a bit more," I said. "In fact, we may have to work in tandem at some points. I don't do that very often, but this is a special case. Are you prepared for that?" I wasn't so sure about this, but I felt I had to give Vance some encouragement.

"Yes!" he shot back eagerly—perhaps as eagerly his wife did when she had herself knocked off.

CHAPTER SEVEN

There were, as I said to Vance, a number of ways to pursue this investigation. I could think of three offhand:

1. Try to learn the whereabouts and true function of the Removal Company. Was this Dr. Sanderson really a noble servant of those people who genuinely wished (for whatever reason) to dispatch themselves, or was he merely a con artist? Was there anything suspicious in the high fee he charged Vance for his "services"? (This may sound naive, but in spite of my coughing fit I later came to the conclusion that, if Sanderson was on the up-and-up, he would require both the large wad of dough and the written guarantees from Vance in order to shield himself from the severest punishment our legal system could inflict.) What of the rigmarole with the blindfolds and mysterious location? This could conceivably be explained the same way—or, conversely, could make it harder for anyone to track the Removal Company's operations.

2. Get some background on Elena Cavalieri. Was she what she claimed to be? How did she come to marry Harry Greenway? Who, indeed, was Harry Greenway? Frankly, this avenue of investigation seemed to me the least promising—or, at any rate, the most difficult and time-consuming to follow up. Aside from her fancied resemblance to Katharine Vance, there was nothing at all to connect Elena to the case.

3. Do some background checking on Dr. William Grabhorn. It was he, after all, who had given Katharine Vance that card from the Removal Company. Was there anything suspicious about that? Was he a

regular "channeler" of clients to Sanderson? Even if that were the case, was there anything intrinsically odd about that? The same things that could be said for (or against) Sanderson could be said for Grabhorn: either he was a self-sacrificing idealist or a crook. The fact that, as a psycho-analyst, he was supposed to help his patients overcome depression, suicidal thoughts, or whatever other problems they may have had was not really to the point: some patients weren't curable, and that was all there was to it.

The fundamental point was this: I had to find something—anything—that was not quite right, something that would lead me to believe that this whole Removal Company operation was not what it seemed. One item out of place, and possibly the whole thing would unravel.

I am always one to choose the easiest and simplest solution to a problem. Why not call the Removal Company's number and see what happened? Vance had been spooked almost into a fainting fit when I had first suggested the idea, but that was before he had explained the whole story to me. There couldn't be any reason not to follow up on this now that I knew the background. If, by some chance, the number was still active, I could simply say that I had a "reference" for the Removal Company's services—another client who might cough up a hundred grand to be relieved of the burden of living.

Or I could even offer myself up as the next victim.

I didn't call the number directly, however. Instead, I called Central and asked the switchboard girl to dial it for me.

I could have predicted the outcome.

"The number has been disconnected, sir." She sounded weirdly cheerful, but I guess they're trained to sound like that.

"Is there any forwarding number?" I asked.

"No, sir, I'm sorry."

"Any address given for that number?"

"No, sir."

"All right. Thanks."

So much for that. But it was only what I'd expected.

How I could possibly track down the location of the Removal

Company—or at least its location when Vance and his wife went there a year and a half ago—was another crux. I knew that New York City had published no city directories since 1926; if they had, it might be possible to find Sanderson's place of business. Instead, there was a "Residential Directory" for Manhattan and the Bronx, and as I strolled to the 42nd Street library to consult it I found the following:

There were thirteen Sandersons listed as living in Manhattan in the 1931/32 residential directory; eight men, and five women. None of them were in Murray Hill—but then, he could be living somewhere other than his "office." After a few phone calls, I quickly found that none of them were doctors. Of course, it was highly probable that Sanderson wasn't even his real name. In that case, the residential directory was useless.

This course of inquiry was rapidly proving fruitless. Sanderson was clearly too clever not to cover his tracks. He could be long gone by now—could be in Boston, or Miami, or Chicago, or anywhere else in the country or the world.

I needed to get in touch with someone who actually knew Sanderson, and knew something about his operation. And the person at the moment who fitted that bill, aside from Vance himself, was William Grabhorn.

I called Vance at his uncle's apartment.

"Tell me something about Grabhorn. How did he come into the picture?"

I could hear Vance choking or sputtering. I had already gotten the feeling, from his earlier account, that he didn't care much from Grabhorn—that he perhaps held him directly or indirectly responsible for what happened to his wife. I wasn't far wrong.

"That two-bit Freud! If I could only get my hands around his neck...." More sputtering.

"Settle down, Vance. This is not helping. Tell me anything you know about him. How long had Katharine been seeing him?"

"God, it must have been about two years before her...you know.... It started just after her father...died. I never met the fellow more than once or twice, but I never liked him."

"Why?"

He seemed to have difficulty with that question. "I just don't know—you'll probably think it's my imagination, or because of what happened later.... But he—he just seemed—" Vance could say no more.

"A quack?" I supplied.

"No, not exactly that." Vance was calming down a bit. "I don't know. I guess I just didn't like Katharine seeing him. I didn't think she really needed it. Or maybe"—his voice suddenly got eager, as if he had come up with an inspiration—"maybe it's because she actually seemed *dependent* on him. I remember now once suggesting—just suggesting, mind you!—that she stop seeing him, and she went into such a tantrum.... It was awful...."

"How did she come upon him?"

"Oh, I don't know. I guess he was pretty well-known as an analyst who specialized in cases of depression. And of course he wasn't cheap. His clientele was pretty rarefied. He wasn't going hungry, I can tell you that." Vance's tone was getting rather snide.

"Did he seem to be helping Katharine at all?"

"Oh, I guess so"—grudgingly. "It was up and down. I'll have to confess that he did seem to help her at the beginning—I think she was more suicidal then than she ever had been before...until the end." A hard swallow. "But after a few months I really couldn't see much improvement—not consistently, anyway. I think going to him just became kind of a habit for her—almost like a drug."

"But she liked him—she wanted to keep on seeing him?"

"Yes"—very grudgingly. "Yes, she did."

After a pause: "Can you take me to him?"

Vance seemed confused for a moment. "What do you mean? Now? You want to see him now?"

Patiently: "Yes, I think it would be a good idea to go to Los Angeles and talk with him. And, if you don't mind, can we take a plane? It will be a bit faster than the train."

Vance replied bitterly: "Mr. Scintilla, I don't think I ever want to ride a Pullman again as long as I live."

* * * * * * *

The ride on American Airlines from Floyd Bennett Field in Brooklyn was a three-legged journey, the plane having to refuel in Chicago and Omaha. Landing late in the afternoon at Los Angeles International Airport, we were promptly picked up by the Vances' chauffeur—a lean young man whom Vance didn't bother to introduce to me, but whom he addressed as Jackson—and were on our way to the family home in San Marino.

I had never been in L.A., and hadn't been in California since I'd tagged along with Henry Mencken on his 1920 visit to San Francisco to cover the Democratic National Convention, and to booze it up with that old reprobate George Sterling. As an Easterner, I found the landscape bemusing. Palm trees in the heart of a city are nice if you like that sort of thing; but what struck me most about Los Angeles—aside from the subtropical weather and the architecture it engendered—was, first, its newness compared with the centuries-old East, and, second, its fundamental lack of *focus*. Maybe I was too used to New York, where development was upward rather than outward; but this grotesque sprawl didn't seem unified. It didn't hang together. It was just a sprinkle of juxtaposed communities, each aggressively preserving its own character.

Things changed a bit when we crossed an open patch of ground next to Griffith Park and entered the small, tightly knit community of San Marino. I laughed to myself at the choice of this place for the Vances' residence. No doubt they chose it because of its exclusivity— only the very rich allowed—but I knew that the town had been established only a few decades ago by Henry E. Huntington, Collis's nephew, and there was a rich irony in the fact that Henry Vance, who had bamboozled the Huntington heirs over the Pacific Mail Steamship Company, decided to plant his roots right in their back yard. We drove by the stately museum, library, and botanical gardens on Oxford Street that Henry Huntington had endowed, and not long afterward turned into an immense driveway whose curving, tree-lined path nearly concealed the towering mansion resting importantly at the end of it.

More servants greeted us, quietly and efficiently attending to our bags. Arthur Vance walked right in; only a quick turn of the head indicated that I was to follow. Inside was all elegance—a little overdone, perhaps, and a hodgepodge of architecture, furniture, and ornament, but not quite as tasteless as some of the (very few) New York millionaires' homes I'd been granted the privilege to enter.

I met Mrs. Vance, a very proper, colorless woman who regarded me with a kind of mingled apprehension and distaste, as if it were somehow disreputable for a family of their stature to hire a private detective. Arthur had, of course, notified her of my arrival, and his story was not far from the truth: he claimed that he had found some leads on Katharine's whereabouts and had called in a professional to help on the job. I couldn't tell whether Mrs. Vance really wanted her daughter-in-law found or not; perhaps it was also disreputable for a member of her family, even one only connected by marriage, to have disappeared.

Mrs. Hawley, Katharine's mother, was not present, and somewhat to my surprise I never saw her during my entire stay with the Vances. Arthur explained that her disappointment at not hearing from her daughter had so embittered her that she had lapsed into a kind of depression herself, and was unlikely to be of much help. He had not told her of his suspicions that Katharine might still be alive, lest he get her hopes up only to have them dashed if nothing was found.

Dinner was a quiet, somber affair. Service was only for three: Henry Vance was, inevitably, away on a business trip. Arthur himself seemed to want to get the meal over quickly, and excused us as soon as tact allowed.

"What now, Scintilla?" he asked when we had settled into an upstairs study.

"We should get to work right away. Of course, there's nothing to be done to-night. But I presume you have a phone number and address for Dr. Grabhorn's office?"

"Yes, of course." He had come prepared, and handed me Grabhorn's business card: 1633 Wilshire Boulevard, EXposition 2171. Vance told me the place was near Beverly Hills. I wasn't surprised, given what he had told me about the economic status of Grabhorn's clientele.

"When was the last time you tried to reach him?" I said.

"By telephone?" Vance asked.

"Yes."

He tousled his hair in thought. "Probably not for a year or more. I didn't have any reason to call him, really. Katharine just went to see him—twice a week, driven there by Jackson—and came back."

"Ever been to his office?"

"Yes...but even longer ago than that. I took Katharine there the first time, back in 1929, and then went there maybe once more a little after that. That's all."

Next morning, after breakfast, I set to work. Somehow I wasn't surprised when I learned from the switchboard girl that EXposition 2171 had been disconnected. I asked her how long ago, but she didn't know.

There needn't be anything suspicious about that—Grabhorn could just have moved. Nor was it odd that he wasn't listed in the current Los Angeles white or yellow pages: Vance told me he hadn't been listed even when Katharine had been going to see him. His referrals came strictly by word of mouth.

"Vance, are you up for a drive to Wilshire Boulevard?" I said.

He almost leaped up from his chair in eagerness. "Let's go!"

Jackson didn't like it, but I wanted to be alone for this bit of work, so I had Vance do the driving.

The building labeled 1633 proved to be a compact, three-story office building. We quickly learned from the building management that Grabhorn—who had occupied the entire second story of the place— had left just about a year ago. No forwarding address.

That was a little odd.

Vance jumped on it. "There's something funny here, Scintilla! What's going on? Where did he vanish to? *And why?*"

"Vance, calm down. It could mean anything."

"But it was just after Katharine's...you know, her...."

"Well, not exactly. It was a good six months after. If he was wanting for some reason to bolt right afterward, surely he wouldn't have hung around another half-year. By the way, I presume he did in fact know what Katharine was going to do?"

"Oh, yes." That bitter sneer again. "She called him just before we left for New York last September. He knew."

"How did he react to it? Do you know?"

"No, I don't. According to Katharine, he just wanted her to do what she felt in her heart she had to do. He didn't try to talk her into it, didn't try to talk her out of it. I guess it didn't please him that he was going to lose a rich patient...unless"—the idea seized Vance with a sudden fury—"unless, by God, that vile Sanderson fellow was giving him some sort of *fee* for his *referrals*...!"

"Vance, you don't know that. You have no business saying that."

"But it stands to reason, Scintilla! God, why didn't I think of it before? Maybe they had this kind of...of *suicide channel* going on...Jesus, what fiends!" Vance was fuming with rage.

"Arthur, just quiet down. It needn't be like that. We still don't know that there's *anything* funny anywhere."

"But where's Grabhorn, then? Where is he?" He was shouting now.

"We'll find him." I turned away and walked out of the building and back to the car. "We'll find him, by God."

CHAPTER EIGHT

It was time to hit the books again.

I had Vance take me to the public library on South Hope Street, where in the immense reference room on the main floor we quickly checked the city directories for the past few years. Sure enough, Grabhorn's office was listed in the directories for 1930 and 1931, but then disappeared. We also discovered his home address for these years—3535 Dahlia Avenue—but this too was dropped from the city directory of 1932. The directory for 1933 had not yet appeared.

I hardly thought it worth the bother to make an investigation of his home address—he had no doubt decamped from there also. Possibly his neighbors might know something, but I doubted it.

I had one more trick up my sleeve. I told Vance:

"Let's go to the Hall of Records—between First and Court Streets, isn't it?"

"Yes," Vance said, a frown wrinkling his face. "But what for? What do you expect to find there?"

"Just take me there and you'll see."

Twenty minutes later we were pulling up in front of the eleven-story gray sandstone and marble building. A helpful girl at the information desk in the lobby directed me to the place I wanted to go: the office where records of legal changes of name were kept.

When Vance learned where we were headed, he was thunderstruck. "You think Grabhorn has changed his name!" He had started it as a question, but by the end it had become a statement of certainty. "By God, that must be it! I *knew* there was something fishy about that devil...."

"Wait a minute, Vance," I cautioned. "This is just a hunch. Maybe it's right, maybe not. But it's just an alternative we have to explore and eliminate."

The clerk in the office—he looked like all clerks in city government: thin, seemingly malnourished, spectacled, and finical—looked at us suspiciously when we entered. I wasted no time stating our business:

"We'd like to look at the file of name changes during the past year or so."

It wasn't going to be that easy; I should have guessed it.

"I'm sorry," he said in a nasal voice, "but that information is not accessible to private individuals. You'll have to get a letter of permission from the Chief of Police or the Board of Supervisors...."

But I had come prepared.

"Sir, I am Joseph Scintilla, Deputy Sheriff of Westchester County, New York. I am on the hunt for a suspected fugitive. Your coöperation would be greatly appreciated."

None of this was a lie. So what if my pal Dan Steeger, Sheriff of Yonkers, had given me the badge as a joke while not entirely sober? I made sure not to use it anywhere near its point of origin, but on occasion it came in handy.

It did the trick. With a faintly resentful "Why didn't you say so in the first place?" the clerk let us walk through the swivel gate and into the office. He momentarily glanced at Vance, perhaps wondering why he hadn't displayed a badge; but Arthur, after a mercifully short look of astonishment, had gained his composure and looked suitably authoritarian, and we marched in as if we owned the place.

The clerk stopped us in front of a wooden cabinet full of drawers, each of them bulging with index cards. He pointed to two drawers and said:

"That's what you want. There must be a thousand or so names there. You may be at it a while, so good luck."

He was about to walk away when I said:

"Say, how are these cards arranged? By the original name of the individual, or the new name?"

Over his shoulder the clerk said: "The new one."

I was afraid of that. The other way would have been a lot simpler. But there was nothing to do but get started. I pulled out both drawers, brought them to a nearby desk, and shoved one in Vance's direction.

"Okay, start looking."

Vance didn't relish the prospect—no more than I did—but he began dutifully enough.

The cards were all handwritten, and were clearly filled out by the persons who were changing their names. It amazed me that there would be so many. If the cards had been arranged by the date of the application, then we might have been in luck: possibly, if Grabhorn had changed his name at all, he might have done so about the time he ditched his home and office a year ago in March. But the cards were arranged alphabetically by the new name, and there was no option but to look through each and every card, looking only at the space where the individual had supplied his old name.

It was about two hours before we came upon it. But we finally did. I was the lucky one.

"Here it is, Vance."

Arthur almost dropped the drawer on his lap in his eagerness to look at the card I was holding up.

"You found him? You found Grabhorn?"

"It sure looks like it. Dr. William Grabhorn is now Dr. William Greer, 623 Prospect Street, Pasadena."

"Pasadena!" Vance almost shrieked. "Why, that's just next to San Marino!"

"Is it? That's interesting. Maybe he wanted to be close to some of his customers."

"But...but why did he change his name? What's going on?"

"It's time to find out, isn't it? Let's give him a call. Or better yet, let's go pay him a visit."

* * * * * * *

We learned from the switchboard girl that Greer's residence was also his place of business. I thought it best not to call, but instead to give him a surprise call in person. We hit the road without delay, and I was kept busy telling Vance to slow down if we expected to reach the place in one piece.

Prospect Street was well-kept, tree-lined, and bounded on both sides with houses whose quiet prosperity was evident to all. Whether or not Dr. William Greer was doing as good a business as a brain-doctor to the wealthy as Dr. William Grabhorn had done, he was not likely to join the queue to the soup kitchen anytime soon. His house was a dignified two-story affair, with two cars in the driveway and one parked on the street in front.

We walked right in. The foyer or lobby was a kind of reception room, and a secretary behind a desk was choosing this idle moment to polish her nails. The nameplate at the front of the desk read: "Lella Cotton." At our abrupt entrance she jumped a bit, but quickly regained the composure she was expected to maintain.

"May I help you?"

"We'd like see Dr. Greer, please," I said. I saw behind her a door with the word "PRIVATE" on it. I could barely make out some muttering behind it.

"I'm afraid Dr. Greer is with a patient right now. You don't have an appointment...?"

I flashed my deputy sheriff's badge and said that I would really be very grateful if Dr. Greer could make some time for me.

At sight of the badge she jumped again a little, then got up. I guess she felt that something like this wasn't suitable for discussion over the intercom.

Opening the "PRIVATE" door barely enough to get into it, she closed it quickly and smartly. I looked at Vance with mild irritation; he looked back at me with a kind of frustrated fury, as though he thought Greer might take the opportunity to climb out a window and elude us.

But Miss Cotton came back pretty fast. Keeping the door open, she waited for an elderly lady in pearls and furs to march in high dudgeon out of the office, then said in a tight little voice: "Dr. Greer will see you now."

I tried not to feel like a patient myself as I walked in, Vance trailing after me.

Dr. William Greer, or Grabhorn, was a big, stocky man—red-faced, bearded, and dressed in a tweed jacket of excellent cut, but which had difficulty embracing his ample girth. He may have been a bit more red-faced than usual, for he was actually huffing with ill-concealed outrage and glaring at us: we could have been some insects that had crawled onto his dinner plate.

"Gentlemen, this is most irregular! I don't know what you mean by barging in like this.... If you weren't officers of the law, I'd have a good mind to...."

I ignored him completely and turned to Vance. "Is that him?"

Vance nodded grimly. "That's him."

I turned back to the doctor, who was so astounded at our disregard of his undoubted importance that he had stopped speaking. "Are you, or were you once known as, Dr. William Grabhorn?"

At the mention of the name I thought the doctor was about to faint. His red cheeks blanched as if a child had colored them over with a crayon, and he could hardly utter. "Wh—what do you...who are you? What do you want from me?"

I decided to press my advantage by playing my trump card. Reaching into my pocket and pulling out the card for the Removal Company, I said: "Do you recognize this?"

The doctor's knees gave way and he would have fallen to the floor if his desk chair hadn't been behind him. "Oh, God...! Why can't you people leave me alone? What have I done...?" I actually thought he was going to cry, but he pulled out his handkerchief only to mop his moistened brow.

"Doctor, I'm a deputy sheriff from Westchester County, New York. This man is Arthur Vance. I take it you are William Grabhorn. Do you recall treating his wife, Katharine Vance?"

Grabhorn looked up at me with a curious expression—confusion mingled with a kind of relief. "Y-yes...yes, of course. I treated her for several years."

"Did you send her to this place?"—holding up the card again.

"No!" The doctor was genuinely angered. "I didn't *send* her there, and I didn't *tell* her to go! My God, but she was in such a bad way!" He gave Vance a quick and apprehensive look. "I tried my best to help her, but it was hopeless! I just thought this might help...."

"Can we see your file on her, doctor?"

At that he stiffened—felt as if he might be able to get the upper hand after all. "You know very well, sheriff, that that file is confidential. You have absolutely no authority—"

"All right, all right," I interrupted quickly. Grabhorn clearly knew what I could and could not do. "I'd just like to know a bit more about the case. We're not accusing you of doing anything wrong. You have committed no crime, so far as we know. But we'd just like to have some information."

Grabhorn was quickly regaining his composure. "All right...although I'm not sure what I can tell you that you probably don't know already." He looked at Vance again. "But sheriff, I really think it best if we talk about this alone. I'm sorry, sir, but—"

Vance exploded. "Not on your life! I'm staying here! She was— is—my wife and I have the right to know! You're going to tell all you can, or—" I thought Vance was going to throttle the doctor, and I quickly grabbed his arm.

"Vance, settle down." He still resisted. "*Settle down*, man. This isn't helping. Maybe the doctor's right."

"I'm just trying to save you some grief, Mr. Vance," Grabhorn said earnestly. "It will be painful...."

Vance's face crumpled into a kind of painful grimace, but he said nothing.

"Vance," I said, "I'll tell you anything of importance that the doctor says. Trust me. You'll know everything that you need to know."

Looking at Grabhorn and me in turn, with a harried, hunted look, Vance abruptly turned on his heel and walked out of the room, slamming the door.

Grabhorn continued the mopping up operations on his face. "He's...he's a bit excitable, isn't he?"

"Perhaps he has reason to be," I said.

"Perhaps."

Grabhorn reached over into a cabinet and took out a bottle of scotch. "Drink?"

"That might be a good idea."

He poured out the liquor—quite a bit of it—into two glasses

brimming with ice, then handed me one.

"So what do you want to know?"

"Everything...everything about Katharine Vance, and everything you know about the Removal Company."

Grabhorn rubbed his chin in a gesture strangely reminiscent of Vance himself. "As I said, I'm not sure I have all that much to tell. But I'll tell it."

This is what he said.

CHAPTER NINE

Katharine Vance was one of my most perplexing cases. I never knew a woman so determined to be unhappy. Perhaps it would be best to say that, even when she should have been happy, she had a knack of seeing the depressing side of things. Although, unlike you or me, she never had to work a day in her life, she didn't find any comfort in her privileged status—in fact, she came to feel strangely ashamed of it.

I never got to know much about her childhood, even though I asked her repeatedly to tell me of it. She was very reticent on some subjects. All I could glean was that from infancy she idolized her father—as only a little girl can idolize a successful and self-confident parent. I don't say that she in any way disliked her mother; she was quite close to her, but that was largely because (so it seemed to me) the two of them both shared this reverence for Mr. Hawley.

Anyway, she seemed to be a lonely child, made friends with difficulty, and spent much of her time wandering by herself on her estate. Throughout her life she never found any compelling interest: various enthusiasms would come and go, but nothing would stick. She was somehow overwhelmed by the futility of her existence—perhaps of all human existence. Everything seemed so pointless to her.

The death of her father was the central, and catastrophic, event of her life. It was, of course, shortly afterward that she was brought in to see me. Mr. Hawley had been forced into speculation in stocks as a result of the increasing extravagance of his family's lifestyle, and he lost pretty much everything in the crash—all except the property on his estate, which was indeed considerable. And yet, having to sell the property and move into a smaller (but still, by any normal person's standards, quite comfortable) quarters was a blow to the entire family, and especially to Katharine. It was not that she missed the luxury; in fact, she had always felt that she didn't deserve it. And now that it was largely gone, she came to believe that it was some kind of punishment for "living off of others," as she called it.

As you are no doubt aware, she marred Arthur Vance not long after that. I don't doubt that she cared for him—he had been a family friend from way back—but the rather hastily arranged union was a further blow to her self-esteem. She felt as if she were some kind of property that was being hawked about from one party to another. It was of course an "advantageous match," but that's exactly what was wrong with it, from Katharine's point of view.

I'll be honest with you, Mr. Scintilla, and say that I'm not entirely sure that Arthur Vance was the right husband for her. Oh, of course he loved her—rather desperately, it seems—but he never understood her. He never realized that Katharine needed to be left alone at times; I think he smothered her with affection, and actually deepened her depression. No doubt that was partly why she had her affair.

Yes, that's right—she had an affair, scarcely less than a year after she was married. You'll of course understand if I don't mention the other man—he was merely another member of their social circle, and he was married also. Katharine told me all about it: told me, in fact, before it began that she was resolved to do something of the kind. It didn't seem to matter with whom it was to be done; it was just something to do. Perhaps she felt that the covertness, the secrecy, the forbiddenness of the thing would appeal to her, lend her some interest in life. Well, it did—for a while. But as you know, these things rapidly become merely cheap, tawdry, and—worst of all—boring and repetitive. It was, in fact, not very difficult for her to conduct the affair, since Arthur was at this time working long hours at his father's office, learning the ropes for his eventual succession to the control of the firm. There was no challenge in it for Katharine—it was too easy, and therefore not a thrill. Frankly, I never chastised her for it—that wasn't my rôle in any case—and I knew it would end soon. It did.

So there it was. I'll admit that Katharine Vance was one of my genuine failures—you mustn't assume that I want all my patients to end as she did! The fundamental point, though, is that *I never seemed to have any effect on her.* Sometimes she felt tolerably well, other times (most of the time, in all honesty) not; but my counseling seemed to make no difference one way or the other. It was most perplexing—I don't even know why she kept on seeing me. In fact, I even told her point-blank that perhaps she should stop doing so, as I didn't seem to be helping her appreciably—but she reacted with such alarm and even *fear* that I quickly backed off from the suggestion.

* * * * * * *

What's that? Yes, yes, I'm coming to that—I'm trying to tell this in a way that will make sense.

Well, by the summer of 1931 Katharine was truly in a state of profound depression. I hardly knew what more to do for her, and even mentioned to her mother the possibility of institutionalizing her—but of course that was inconceivable, it would be too great a blow to the family's social standing. In any case, Katharine wasn't *insane* by any definition that we psycho-analysts recognize.

She had been talking about suicide for weeks—more and more determinedly. It became an obsession with her, and there was one session that was largely taken up with her querying me almost maniacally which method might be the most painless. She didn't like pain.

And so I gave her that card for the Removal Company.

What? No, the fellow's name was not Sanderson. He told me it was Kratzner. Just wait a moment—let me tell this my own way.

In 1927—years before I ever treated Katharine Vance—I was at a psychiatric conference in Mamaroneck, New York. I have no idea why it was there—but I'll admit the furnishings at the hotel were comfortable. Anyway, I had just participated in a panel discussion on treating clinical depression when this man approached me, introduced himself, and asked to talk with me in private. He looked harmless enough, so I agreed.

What did he look like? Oh, tall, slim, gray-haired, rather haggard but very intelligent-looking face. Does that sound right? Okay. Well, I simply led him to a small conference room that wasn't being used at the moment, and we sat down. Now of course I can't remember now exactly what he said, but it went something like this:

"Doctor Grabhorn, I greatly admired your discussion today. It is evident that you have treated many cases of depression—am I right?" His voice was very soft, controlled, well-modulated.

"Yes, indeed. It is my specialty," I said.

"I wonder," he said, in a kind of wistful way, "what you do with cases that you find...shall we say, difficult?" He made it sound as if it were a purely theoretical question.

"Almost all cases of depression are difficult, Dr. Kratzner."

"Yes, no doubt, no doubt...." A strange sort of smile played on his lips. "Perhaps there are cases that are, indeed, hopeless—insoluble?"

"I'm sure there are." I really didn't know where this was going. Was he wanting me to treat someone?—perhaps himself?

"What would you do in such a case?" he asked. "Stop treatment?"

"If," I said, "there seemed no point in continuing sessions with the depressed patient, then I would at least suggest to the patient that we cease. But if the patient wishes to continue, then I would do so. I would think that some kind of treatment is better than none."

"No doubt, no doubt," he said again, and trailed off.

Somewhat abruptly—it was the only abrupt move I ever saw him make—he got up and began walking about in a small circle.

"Doctor Grabhorn," he said, "let me be plain. I offer a distinctive kind of service for certain kinds of patients. Indeed, let us not call them patients at all—the term is so...clinical, no? Let us just say, certain individuals."

I have to confess that my immediate thought was that he was some kind of quack. "Exactly what service do you offer?" I asked.

"A very delicate one...very delicate. To be blunt, doctor, I assist people in ridding themselves of their unwanted lives."

I was thunderstruck. Was this some kind of joke?

"What the hell do you mean?" I exploded. "You mean mercy killing? You end the lives of people who are terminally ill?"

"Calm yourself, doctor," he said, holding up one hand gently. "It is not perhaps what you think. I do not restrict myself only to the terminally ill. I am of the opinion that anyone, in whatever condition of body or mind, who wishes to depart from life should be allowed to do so. Surely you do not believe that persons should be forced to continue an existence they find distasteful?"

"Well, no, of course not—if that's what they really want to do...." I was still reeling from this man's bizarre story.

"Please do not misunderstand me," Kratzner said. "I neither encourage nor discourage people in their actions. I do not, strictly speaking, seek clients, but if a client wishes to come to me and is truly resolved upon his course of action, then I provide assistance. Is that so terrible?"

That bland, emotionless face was bothering me. Was this person a charlatan, a fiend, or in fact a savior? As I sat there irresolute, Kratzner continued:

"I think you might find some reassurance from Doctor—" he mentioned a name—a very prominent name in our field. "He knows my work quite well, and I believe he can provide a reference."

No, Scintilla, I won't tell you. *I won't tell you, do you hear?* That doctor is still exceptionally well known, and moreover is a close friend of mine; and I *will not* give him away. It is not any of your affair—you have no business with him.

Anyway, that name certainly gave me food for thought. Kratzner didn't say much more, but before he left he did hand me a small stack of those business cards—just like the one you have. All he said was:

"In the event that you have a patient who might perhaps benefit from my services...."

And then he left.

Well, I didn't waste time. I called that doctor friend of mine, and he vouched for Kratzner fully. He said he had visited Kratzner's "office" in New York and found it entirely above-board, decent, and civilized. Of course, my doctor friend was quite aware that what Kratzner was doing was illegal, but my friend was devoted to individual freedom and felt the state had no business interfering with decisions of that sort. If you're worried that any large number of people will kill themselves if the means to do so are made easy for them, think again. I've known many depressed people who made me wonder how they managed to live another day without resorting to suicide; only a tiny fraction of them would ever do so—and even a smaller fraction of the general public. The love of life—or shall we say the fear of death—is too well ingrained in people. Suicide is simply not an option: the great majority of individuals will continue to drag out their existence no matter how wretched they are.

So perhaps there is a use for that Removal Company.

The point is that it never occurred to me to "recommend" anyone for Kratzner's services until I treated Katharine Vance and saw, toward the end, how completely despondent she was. She talked about suicide all the time—all the time. Don't come back with that canard that anyone who talks about suicide won't do it; that's too simple-minded a formulation. Anyway, all I did was to suggest that Katharine check out this place; she was under no obligation to make actual use of the service. At all times it would be her decision to make.

What's that? No, I never saw Kratzner again, and I never went to his "office." I never even called that number myself—I knew from my friend that Kratzner was in New York, and beyond that I didn't care much. There's no reason why I should have. I had never recommended anyone to the Removal Company before, and I never did so again. Not because I had any difficulty, moral or otherwise, with what he was doing, but because no other of my patients seemed suitable for it.

And that's all I know, Mr. Scintilla. That's entirely all.

CHAPTER TEN

To my surprise, I found Vance not in the doctor's lobby—where the receptionist, with apparently not a shred of work to do, had resumed the beautifying of her nails—but outside, pacing on the sidewalk and still fuming. When I appeared, he gave me a look of what some might have thought pure hatred, but very quickly it turned to a kind of mingled eagerness and inquiry.

"What happened?" he snapped. "What did he say? Does he know Sanderson?—does he know where we can reach him?"

"Take it easy, Vance," I said, as we both climbed into the car. "He's given me a lot to chew on."

On the drive back home I told him pretty much everything that Grabhorn had said—leaving out the part about Katharine's affair, and a few other things. I had also asked Grabhorn what had led him to change his name, but he had merely come back with the standard "That's my affair, not yours," so there wasn't much I could do with that.

So what was Grabhorn/Greer's game, anyway? Was the name change a way to evade the police? From everything I had learned, Sanderson/Kratzner was exceptionally careful about keeping his operation a secret, so Grabhorn didn't seem to have any compelling reason to take cover, especially in such a cumbersome manner. Changing your name causes all sorts of complications, and it's not something a person does lightly. Even if he had managed to keep his wealthy clientele—as the pearled and furred lady whose session we had so rudely interrupted seemed to suggest—he had had to uproot himself both from his former home and his place of business, and there must have been a great many other inconveniences.

So what was he running from?

And how much was I to believe his story? All of it, some of it, or none? The parts about Katharine Vance—even the affair—rang true, and fitted with what I had learned from other sources. But that wasn't the important part: we knew already that she was suicidal, and no one was claiming that Grabhorn or even Sanderson had somehow pressured her into her final act. It was entirely voluntary; our two doctor friends had just paved the way, and—unless you were the police—there was nothing intrinsically wrong with that. So on this point, I still had nothing to go on—nothing that I could consider a "case."

How about his meeting with Sanderson at that conference? That sounded okay—at any rate, I had no reason to disbelieve it. The real crux centered on three points:

1) Was Grabhorn telling the truth when he said that Katharine Vance was the only person he had ever recommended to the Removal Company?

2) A related point: Did Grabhorn really have no further contact with the Removal Company?

3) Most important of all: Who was this other doctor—a leading figure in his field—who had vouched for Sanderson?

That was something I had to find out. It might—*might*—be the key to the unraveling of the matter, if there was anything to unravel.

There seemed only one way to get to the bottom of these three puzzles. I would have to pay an uninvited call to Dr. Grabhorn/Greer's office and do some snooping. There seemed no better time than this evening.

I knew I had to leave Arthur Vance out of it. He was too excitable, and this kind of investigation was better done alone. If by chance I got caught, it was better that only one person get in trouble with the police than two.

I am one of those rare New Yorkers who actually know how to drive a car; it comes in handy in my work. So after dinner I made a point of requesting one of the several cars owned by the Vances, saying that I needed it to pursue some private investigations. Vance himself was surprisingly indifferent on the point, merely throwing me the keys of the Aston Martin we had taken to Grabhorn's office. I would have preferred something a bit less conspicuous, but I wasn't planning on having Grabhorn or anyone else see me at my work.

I left around 9 P.M., knowing that I would have to wait until at least after midnight before I could take any action. It was a shame that Grabhorn's office was also his residence; but on the other hand, a private house is far easier to break into than an office building. The placidly suburban environment was a perfect cover, too: the neighbors would—as suburbanites are—be so unused to burglars that they were not likely to be very vigilant.

So I drove around for several hours—getting the lay of the land, stopping by at an all-night cafe in San Gabriel for coffee and doughnuts, even heading as far as Hollywood to eye the starlets, the whores (hard to tell the difference sometimes), and the gaping tourists. I decided not to press on to Beverly Hills: I'd already had my fill of extravagant luxury at the Vances'.

Half an hour past midnight saw me pull up to about two blocks from Grabhorn's house. I parked the car on the sidewalk and calmly walked to my destination. Everything was dead quiet—no illumination anywhere except on infrequent street-lights. I had made sure to wear dark clothing.

Grabhorn's place also seemed entirely dead—not a sound, light, or movement. I assumed that his bedroom was upstairs, and thought it likely that he would be sound asleep. No doubt the receptionist was long gone.

From my memory of the layout, his office was in the back, and there was a window there—rather small and high up, but probably serviceable. I went around back and stood in front of it; it wasn't latched. Bringing out my crowbar, I lodged it carefully at the bottom pane of the window—freezing a moment when I heard a car drive by, although I saw no headlights—and pried it up. It creaked a bit at first, so I stopped for a moment and, as soon as I could get my fingers under it, continued to push it up slowly.

It was, as I say, a high window—probably five feet from the

ground. Its width was scarcely two feet. I'm not the most athletic person imaginable, but I managed to lever myself up to the window-ledge, hang there on my stomach while I gained my balance, and then fall clumsily into the room, landing heavily, but without much noise, on the thick couch under the window. So far, so good.

Grabhorn's file cabinets occupied the entire back wall of the office—there were at least six of them. I didn't know where to start, and suspected that I might be in for a long evening. Pulling out my flashlight, I shone it on the placards in front of one of the file drawers, but I couldn't make any sense of it—it was in some kind of private code or system of organization that Grabhorn used.

I pulled the drawer. It didn't budge.

I gave an almost audible sigh of disgust. How tedious! It was locked. I confess that I've never been good at lock-picking, but if I have enough time I can usually manage. I fished my pick out of my pocket and began to work.

Then I heard—or thought I heard—some movement upstairs.

It sounded something like a thud—possibly someone getting up heavily from bed and placing his foot hard on the floor. I first closed the window by which I had come in, then looked quickly around the room. Aside from the door leading out into the lobby, there was only one other door, framed between two immense bookshelves. I went to it and opened it carefully. It was a bathroom. I don't know why I was surprised, but I was.

I stood entirely still, straining my ears. If the need for concealment arose, this bathroom would do in a pinch. Aside from the large desk, there was scarcely any furniture that would provide much cover, and the room seemed to have no closet.

But I heard no further sound. Possibly Grabhorn merely had to use the bathroom upstairs, although I heard no footsteps walking to and fro.

After several minutes of complete silence I resumed my work. The lock was not easy to pick, or else my skills weren't quite up to the job. But I kept at it.

Then I heard the explosion.

It could only be one thing—a large-caliber gun going off inside a house. Only that could make the kind of heart-thumping, teeth-chattering noise that I heard. I wheeled around, somehow expecting the gunman to be standing at the door—maybe even expecting to feel the bullet enter my own body. But the gun had clearly gone off upstairs.

Within half a minute of the gunshot, I heard a police siren rapidly approaching the house. This was not good. It was time for me to get out of here.

I pried open the window, levered myself out—even more clumsily than before—and landed heavily on the wet grass outside. For a moment the wind was knocked out of me, but I recovered quickly. Slamming down the window, I bolted for my waiting car.

Reaching there without incident, I heard the police car coming ever closer. It was unmistakably heading for the Grabhorn house. I felt I had to investigate—something queer was going on. So I got in the car and drove the two blocks to the house.

The police car had already pulled up, and the door of the house was open—probably broken down by the officers. Not long afterward at least two other cars wheeled around the street corner and bore down upon us. Several police officers and what looked like a plainclothes detective stormed out of their vehicles.

By this time I had sidled my car to the kerb of the house opposite Grabhorn's. I was not entirely sure when I should make my own presence known, if at all. I got out of the car calmly and quietly. One policeman was standing guard outside the house. I approached him.

"Sir, this is a crime scene," he said, officiously. "Please stay back. You'd better just go home."

I flashed my badge. "Deputy Sheriff, Westchester County," was all I said.

The policeman looked puzzled, and that made him let his guard down a bit. I chose that moment to walk into the place.

I saw a man who appeared to be the detective in charge—as much in charge as anyone could be given the circumstances. He glared at me with a kind of outrage until I did my badge routine again. Quick introductions followed; he turned out to have the incredible name of Gulliver Crane.

"Detective Crane, can I ask what has happened?" I said.

He looked at me closely. It was clear he didn't know what to make of me. "Deputy, may I ask exactly what your business is here?"

I knew, of course, that I had no authority here; this whole matter was entirely under the jurisdiction of the Pasadena police department. It was advisable to be courteous and deferential.

"Sir, I am pursuing a private investigation regarding Dr. William Greer. I am not at liberty to reveal more. I'd just like some information as to what's going on."

This didn't satisfy him.

"I don't know what you're up to, Sheriff Scintilla, but I think you're a bit out of your depth here. Dr. William Greer has been murdered."

Somehow I had expected that.

"Do you know who's responsible?" I said.

At that moment I heard several officers engaged in a fierce tussle with someone as they were trying to herd him downstairs. The man was putting up a good fight, but the policemen finally managed to subdue him. He was already handcuffed, and with some difficulty they led him to one of the police cars and stuffed him in.

"That's our man, I think," Sargent said with some satisfaction.

The man they had put into the police car was Arthur Vance.

CHAPTER ELEVEN

"Vance, what's going on?"

It was some hours later, and we were at Pasadena police headquarters. I had not been allowed to investigate the crime scene; indeed, in my continued absence of a convincing explanation for why I was there at all, Detective Crane and his boys were distinctly uncooperative. All I could ascertain was this:

Grabhorn/Greer had been found dead in his bedroom, with a bullet wound—a large one—in his chest. Death was probably instantaneous, but he had suffered another injury to the back of his head when he fell back against the marble mantelpiece of his fireplace: there was blood on the corner of the mantelpiece, presumably where his head had struck it.

Vance, meanwhile, was found in the bedroom, lying on the floor in a rather groggy condition, with the gun—his own—in his hand. The gun had been fired, and subsequent tests revealed that the bullet that had pierced Grabhorn's heart was indeed from this weapon. No other bullets were found, and no other gunshots were heard by anyone. Under the circumstances, it was crazy to think that anyone else had killed Grabhorn.

But Vance adhered to a wild story that he had been struck on the head by someone from behind, and woke up, sitting in the bedroom with the gun in his hand, just as the police entered the house. Sure enough, Vance did have an injury to the back of his head, of the sort that *might* have been made by a blackjack, but could just as well have been the result of a collision of his own against some hard substance.

As for what Vance was doing there in the house at all, he resolutely refused to say. He did not deny that he had come to the house to investigate, even to break in: his roadster had been found only a block away. But, incredibly, Vance maintained that the front door of the house was not merely unlocked, but actually ajar. However, the police found clear evidence of forced entry on the door jamb. Vance had no recollection of going upstairs: he continued to maintain, to Detective Crane's disgust, that he had been waylaid almost as soon as he had entered the place.

It took some sweet-talking for me even to see Vance, who had been booked without delay and was in the holding pen. But I promised Crane that I would give him some account of myself, and of Vance, as soon as I could talk to Vance. Since Arthur wasn't going anywhere—it was highly unlikely that a judge would allow bail to be posted for him—Crane shrugged and let me have my wish. "But you come and see me afterward!" he barked.

I sat myself down on an uncomfortable wooden chair outside the holding pen. Vance was in a kind of brooding fury and didn't answer my first question—hardly paid attention to it. So I repeated it with considerable emphasis:

"Vance, what the hell's going on? What were you doing at that house? Did you kill Grabhorn?"

He ignored that last question. "Well, Scintilla, what were *you* doing there? And why didn't you tell me you were going?"

I was irritated. "Who's running this investigation anyway? I'm still not sure there's anything to investigate—except the possibility that my own client may be guilty of murder—but I'll be damned if I come running to you like a schoolboy every time I want to do anything."

I was getting angrier by the minute. "And now look what you've done! You bloody fool!—I was on the verge of finding out something, and you had to go blow the fellow away. He was harmless, and probably didn't even know anything—"

Vance roared: *"I didn't kill him!"*

I was silent for a moment. Each of us fumed at the other.

I said very quietly: "You expect me to believe this cockamamie story of you being hit on the head as you walked into an open front door, and then waking up to find yourself sitting in Grabhorn's room with a gun—*your* gun—in your hand and the good doctor with a hole in his chest? Come off it, Vance. If you tell that story in court you needn't wait for the electric chair to fry your eyes out."

With an inarticulate shriek Vance lunged at me, reaching his hands through the bars and almost grabbing my head. With an agility I didn't know I had I leaped backward off the chair, upsetting it and nearly falling to the ground. The police guard, half asleep, jerked himself into action and with a billy club forced Vance to retreat.

"You all right, mister?" the guard asked.

"Yeah, I'm fine," I said, dusting myself off. He looked at both me and Vance a little apprehensively, but I assured him: "It's all right. Just leave us alone. We'll be okay."

The guard shrugged and resumed his position near the door.

"Vance," I said, "we're both tired and upset. This is not what we bargained for. For the life of me I can't figure out why anyone would want to bump Grabhorn off and try to frame you for it. There's something very strange going on here...."

Vance, who had been in a furious sulk, suddenly beamed with eagerness. "I've been trying to tell you that all along! Didn't I say there was something funny about this Removal Company?"

"Oh, Vance, knock it off. How in hell do you think this Sanderson or Kratzner fellow had anything to do with this? The last time anyone knew, he was in New York."

"Well, maybe he's here now! Maybe he knows that I'm trying to track him down, and...and...."

"How?"

As on several previous occasions, Vance was brought up short. "What do you mean, how?"

"How does Sanderson know about you—or us?"

Vance looked around his small cage as if an answer might be lurking in some dim corner. "Oh, God knows, Scintilla. That man might be capable of anything! I tell you he's some kind of fiend...."

"Oh, pipe down, Vance." I was fed up with him and his wild theories. Maybe he was right—anything was possible—but there was no proof, no evidence, not even the faintest trace of it.

I tried another tack. "What exactly were you doing in that house, anyway?"

Vance looked huffy. "Same as you, Scintilla: trying to find out something. You're not the only one who can snoop around."

"Why didn't you leave that to me? Isn't that why you hired me?"

"Look, you have your ways, and I have mine! I didn't know you were going to do exactly what I was doing. Why didn't you tell me?"

"Frankly," I said, "I didn't want you tagging along. It's pretty obvious that you're not in control of yourself."

"Oh, Scintilla, get off my case! I was perfectly in control until I got quashed on the head. *None of this is my fault, damn it!*"

"All right," I said tiredly. "All right. But what now? I'll take your word for it that you didn't kill Grabhorn, although for the life of me I can't imagine who else could have. But what do I do now?"

Vance looked at me as if I were an imbecile. "Why, just go on with the investigation! Now you clearly have something to investigate: as you say, something strange is definitely going on. Hunt down this other doctor who recommended the Removal Company; find out who Mrs. Harry Greenway is, or was. Don't worry about me; I'll get out of this mess somehow."

His own fate seemed a matter of complete indifference to Vance. It was admirable, I suppose—assuming that there was nothing peculiar behind it.

I was about to go, when one more point occurred to me. "You still maintain that you found the door of the house open? You didn't break in?"

"No." Vance, teeth gritted, was emphatic. "It was *open.* I just walked in."

"The police say they found clear marks that the door was jimmied. You didn't do that?"

"Absolutely not."

As a matter of fact I hadn't heard any sound of the front door being jimmied when I was in Grabhorn's office. Would I have? That office door was pretty heavy. I certainly wouldn't have heard Vance—or anyone else—walk upstairs, because of the thick carpeting in both the foyer and the staircase.

I left shortly thereafter. By this time it was nearly 3:30 in the morning, but you'd never know that from the way the police department was hopping over this murder case. I trudged upstairs and knocked on Detective Crane's door, and was greeted with a gruff: "Come in!"

Our talk was not very conclusive. I still didn't know how much to tell him, and that may have made me come off as suspicious. Crane was struck, however, by my discovery of Grabhorn's change of name: he hadn't known that, and it gave him food for thought.

"But I don't see how that affects this shooting, Scintilla," Crane said. "By whatever name Greer was going by, he was still shot by Vance."

"My client says he didn't do it." I guess I didn't sound very convinced; maybe because I wasn't.

"Yeah, well, he can also say that he's been to the moon and back: that doesn't mean I'll believe him. I know who he is, Scintilla: I know his father is Mister Moneybags, but that don't make a bit of difference to me. If he's guilty—and he is—then he's going down."

"Okay, fine. He's only my client, he's not my brother." I was getting a bit of a headache. "Let me ask you this, Detective: How did your men get to that house so quickly? They must have arrived within a minute or two of the shooting."

Crane was prepared for that. "We got a tip—claiming to be from a neighbor, although she didn't identify herself—that someone was breaking into the house. So we sent a squad car over there at once. You know that area, Scintilla"—Crane broke into a crooked grin—"these people like to be protected: they have too much to lose from burglars. So when that car was on its way, the officers heard the shot and immediately called in for reinforcements. I was here when that call came through, so I decided to take charge."

I said nothing to all this. Whether the anonymous neighbor had seen me or Vance was not something I wanted Crane to clarify.

There was not much more I could do here. Vance could fend for himself: he had the resources to do so. If he wanted me to continue the investigation, I would. But I was pretty much stymied at this end: Crane would surely not allow me to look through Grabhorn's papers now, so finding that doctor friend of his who had recommended the

Removal Company was out of the question.

It was time to head back to New York. I wanted to see what I could find out about Mr. and Mrs. Harry Greenway.

CHAPTER TWELVE

It was good to be on familiar turf again.

Los Angeles was fine if you had a car and liked the beach, but for one accustomed to the frenetic pace of crowded Eastern cities it was as alien as the steppes of Russia. I liked being able to go anywhere I needed to go by subway, elevated, bus, ferry, or (when I felt extravagant) taxi. I liked the fact that my corner deli had nearly everything I needed for my frugal meals, that my post office, stationery store, drugstore, even police station were within walking distance of home or office.

And, I have to confess, I was more than a little relieved that I was away from the oppressive presence of Arthur Vance. Not many clients in the past had thrown money my way so insouciantly, but I was now glad that he would be in cold storage for a while, a continent away. There was something about him that was beginning to bother me.

At first I had felt sorry for him: he was clearly wrought up over his wife's death—if that's what it was—and seemed desperate to prove, at least to himself, that it had all been some mistake. Maybe he half knew—what I had learned from the late Dr. Grabhorn—that he had not been as much of a help to Katharine in her various times of need as he had hoped; that, in fact, he may have had no small part in driving her to her ultimate act. That would have been a pretty tough thing to take for a man not yet thirty.

But now I was beginning to look at him in a different way. Perhaps, in my prejudice against the wealthy—especially the sons and daughters of the wealthy—I had underestimated his intellect and cunning. What was his game, if he had a game? I had taken practically everything he said at face value. Was his excitable, nervous temperament—bordering on hysteria, it seemed to my unprofessional medical opinion—simply an act? Was he actually manipulating me toward some unfathomable end?

And did he, or did he not, kill William Grabhorn? What could he possibly have to gain by doing so? Did Grabhorn know something about Vance that Vance couldn't afford to have known?

Well, I didn't have the answers to any of these questions. But I was glad to have a little distance from him for a while. From now on, he himself would be among my suspects.

Right now, however, my concern was with Elena Cavalieri. As before, I needed to find something—anything—that would indicate some flaw, some cover-up in her background. If, in even the smallest particular, she was something other than what she said she was, I might have something to work with.

Some of the background work I could do myself. That chap on the *Herald-Tribune*, Gene Merriwether, might be a start.

I sauntered over to the *Herald-Tribune* offices on West 41st Street and asked for him at the front desk. The officious male receptionist, looking more like a police officer than a compatriot of that nails-obsessed beauty at Grabhorn's office, gave me the once-over and grudgingly barked out directions to the fifth floor.

Merriwether was a prepossessing young man, looking even younger than Arthur Vance although they had to be pretty much the same age. He was clean-cut, eager to please, a little harried, and trying to conceal the fact that the society columns of even a major newspaper were not exactly where he felt his talents to lie.

After I had announced my mission, he perked up considerably. Maybe he thought this matter might somehow work to his credit. But in all fairness, his primary wish was to help his friend Vance.

"Yes, Mr. Scintilla, I sent him that clipping." He suddenly turned rueful. "I hope to heaven I haven't caused more problems than before. I knew he was awful upset about Katharine's leaving him. And I really didn't mean to upset him."

"Well, he was pretty upset," I said bluntly.

Merriwether winced. "I'm sorry to hear that. He's really one of my best friends."

"I don't doubt it." I shifted gears. "Tell me what led you to fancy a resemblance between Katharine Vance and this Elena Cavalieri woman."

"Well, there *is* a resemblance," Merriwether said, a bit desperately. "A *great* resemblance."

"All right, let's say there is. But what would lead you to think that Elena Cavalieri was Katharine Vance?"

"Oh, I didn't say that! I just thought Arthur would be interested in the resemblance...."

There was something odd here. "Did Arthur tell you what had happened between him and Katharine?"

Merriwether shifted uncomfortably in his uncomfortable chair. "Well, not very much. He just said Katharine had decided to leave him—that her mind was made up, and that there was nothing anybody could do about it."

So Vance hadn't told Merriwether about the whole business with the Removal Company. That made sense: if he hadn't told even his family, he wasn't likely to tell even a good friend.

"I think Arthur even said that the blow-up had happened in New York—which surprised me, because he had made no effort to look me up when he was here. I was rather hurt by that—I hadn't seen him for years."

"What did he say to that?"

"Oh," Merriwether waved his hand irresolutely, "just that they'd been pretty busy and didn't have time to look up anyone. It didn't convince me, although I did learn that he never saw any of our other friends here, either." He refocused himself. "You see, what's why I thought that maybe this Elena woman really was, or might be, Katharine. I mean, Katharine had totally disappeared! If she had stayed in New York, maybe she had changed her name, or something—you know, started her life all over again. She was still pretty young...."

"When did you last see her?"

"Katharine? Well, I guess it would have been around 1927, when I came back home for a visit. I don't have much of a chance to get away, you know...."

I was startled. "That was six years ago—and four years before Katharine and Arthur Vance...er, split up."

Merriwether wriggled some more. "Yes, I know. It *was* a long time. But you don't forget a face like Katharine's! Anyway, remember that I wasn't really saying this Elena *was* Katharine, just that she *looked* like her...." He trailed off indecisively.

"Okay, fine." This wasn't getting me anywhere. "Just what do you know about Elena Cavalieri—now Mrs. Harry Greenway?"

"Well, not very much...." Merriwether looked down at his shoes. Then suddenly he perked up again. "But, say! I know someone who might! Just sit tight, okay, Mr. Scintilla—I'll be right back."

And before I could say or do anything he had hopped up from his chair and retreated into the bowels of the *Herald-Tribune* offices.

In a surprisingly short amount of time he had in tow a slim, curvy young woman, quite good-looking, hair tied up in a bun, whose only blemish was the immense wad of gum she was chewing. She had a notepad in her hand and was giving Merriwether an irritated look as he almost dragged her to where we were seated.

"Mr. Scintilla, this is Marge Schaeffer," Merriwether said. "She works in our department also."

"Pleased to meetcha," Marge said somewhat coldly, as if her annoyance with her colleague had transferred itself to its apparent source.

"Marge wrote that piece on the Greenway marriage, didn't you, Marge?" Merriwether said, in a kind of desperate eagerness.

"Sure I did." More gum chewing.

"So you've met Elena Cavalieri—Mrs. Greenway?" I asked.

"Sure." This Schaeffer woman seemed to be about the most ill-bred society reporter I'd ever met. "A couple of times."

"Do you mind answering some questions about her?"

"No, I suppose not." At this point Merriwether almost pushed Marge into the chair he had been occupying, hovering behind her like a guardian angel.

"So Elena Cavalieri came from Italy?" I asked.

"Well, sure"—as if I were a fool. "God knows she had a pretty heavy Italian accent when I talked to her—that was about a week before the marriage. Said she was a second cousin of Harry Greenway, had come to stay with the family earlier that year—maybe in January—and they'd fallen in love. Her parents had died recently—that was why she'd come over from Italy, and that's why no family was mentioned in that write-up. You know, we usually mention both the bride's and the groom's parents in our notices, but she didn't want to talk about her parents—she was still pretty cut up about them. And that's all I know."

That was quite a bit. A lot to mull over. I had been frantically writing down what Marge had been saying—she made no allowance for my slowness in dictation—and was still writing several moments after she had finished. So she sat chewing her gum and looking blandly at me as I scribbled.

When I finished I said, "That's a big help, Miss Schaeffer. A big help."

Finally she cracked a smile. "You don't say? Well, glad to be of service." She sprung up from the chair and began to march off, then stopped abruptly and turned around.

"Is there something funny going on with her—with Elena Greenway?"

I looked up at her. "I wish I knew."

* * * * * * *

There were some things I could check right away. One bit I could find by walking only a couple of blocks from where I had been sitting: Room 328—the Genealogical Reading Room—of the New York Public Library on 42nd Street.

I was comfortable in this library. Don't get the impression I'm a bookworm: I may have studied philosophy at Johns Hopkins, but I quickly realized that the whole history of philosophy, and perhaps of all human endeavor, was one long comedy of errors. No; that's not why I haunted this place. There was more information—hard, practical information—here than most people could even begin to fathom; you just had to know where to find it. Between census reports, city directories, telephone books, detailed maps of every corner of the city, and— my current interest—genealogical records, there were all sorts of nuggets that had been instrumental to my work in the past. I hoped it would be today.

Genealogy wasn't my specialty, so I needed some help from the librarians, which they were only too ready to supply. They told me that there was actually a published genealogy of the Greenway family: it had come out about thirty years ago, and was on the open shelf. I found it without difficulty and examined it.

Harry Greenway came from a family whose primary wealth—and it was considerable—had come from shipping. The family owned a significant proportion of the freighters that brought products into New York from European ports, and it was pretty prominent in the city's social life as well. Harry Greenway was by no means young—according to the genealogy, he would by now be about fifty-five. The point was: Did he have some relation to the Cavalieri family?

Rather to my astonishment, he did. The genealogy I was consulting was published too early to include Elena, but it definitely listed an Ettore and Sophia Cavalieri as first cousins, making their daughter Elena (if that was who she was) Harry's second cousin.

Imagine that. If there had been anything in what Arthur Vance had been saying—if it really was the case that Katharine Vance had somehow not died, but had remade herself as Elena Cavalieri—then you would have thought that this whole story of her being a cousin of the Greenways would have been a fiction, and that would have started the whole house of cards tumbling down.

I will confess that this matter jolted me. I had actually come to think that there *was* something funny going on, and—in spite of my faint but burgeoning suspicions of Arthur Vance himself—that this Elena Cavalieri was not what she seemed. Or maybe I was just *hoping* for something out of the ordinary.

Well, I wasn't going to let the matter rest. One might as well be thorough—that's what Vance was paying me for, anyway. There was one more expedition I had to take.

Taking the Seventh Avenue subway to South Ferry, I boarded the ferry to go to Ellis Island.

The sea was choppy that day, and I am not comfortable when not on solid ground, so the trip, although lasting only twenty minutes, was not pleasant. But as soon as I found myself on the E-shaped island I made my way quickly to the immigration office. I had a pal—well, let's say a distant acquaintance—named Ambrose Wheeling; he had helped me a bit in the past, and hoped he might be able to do so now.

He could. With a careless wave of his hand he let me poke through the records of incoming immigrants for 1932. If Marge Schaeffer had been right in saying that Elena had come over in January of that year, her record should be easy to find. If that part of the story was false, then again I might have something to work on—the thread that would untie the skein of deceit (if that's what it was) that Arthur Vance had been convinced had been weaved around his wife.

I was out of luck. Within half an hour I found the immigration record for Elena Cavalieri—she had arrived on the *Rè di Ponto* on January 19, 1932, from Cattolica, Italy. Had come alone, with proper passport and visa. There was even a photograph attached. It was exactly the one in the *Herald-Tribune* clipping about her marriage to Greenway.

By God, this was frustrating! I was now getting to the point of believing that both Vance and I were barking up the wrong tree. There was nothing here: nothing out of place, nothing irregular, nothing false or deceitful about Elena Cavalieri, or Mrs. Harry Greenway. Everything checked out.

At this stage I could only think of one thing to do. I would—if I could manage it—talk to Elena face to face.

CHAPTER THIRTEEN

Marge Schaeffer was not pleased. Evidently the mild interest she had expressed in my investigations had rapidly waned when I had left the *Herald-Tribune* office, and dwindled to the vanishing-point when she realized that she would have to do some extra-curricular work of her own.

"You want me to do what?" she shot back at me in outrage, with Gene Merriwether looking on apprehensively, wringing his hands.

"Miss Schaeffer," I said as calmly as possible, "I would be very grateful for your help in this matter. All I'm asking is that you set up an interview with Mrs. Elena Greenway and discuss certain things with her—mostly about her background."

"Yeah?" she said. "Under what pretext? Do you know what blue-bloods these Greenways are? I can't just barge in and..."

"I'm sure we can think of something," I replied. "Maybe say that you're working on an article on Italian immigrants and their place in the upper tier of New York social life...."

Almost before I could finish she retorted: "We don't do that kind of article here!"

I closed my eyes for a moment. "I think it very unlikely that Mrs. Greenway knows that, don't you think?"

For once this gum-chewing dame was held silent.

Gene broke in: "Marge, it's for a good cause." He made it sound like a charity ball. "My friend Arthur Vance is really in a bad way, and—"

She wheeled on him. "Look, Gene, I don't have the time to help every Tom, Dick, or Harry that gets into trouble! Do you know how much work is piled up on my desk right now?" She turned back to me. "Look, Mr. Scintilla, give it to me straight: Has Mrs. Greenway done anything wrong?"

"Not that I know of."

"She's not in trouble with the police?"

"If she was, presumably the police would be handling it." Maybe that wasn't the smartest thing to say under the circumstances: it made Marge seem foolish. But she didn't seem to notice.

"So then what exactly are you trying to accomplish?"—accusingly.

"I'm just pursuing a line of investigation. Perhaps there's something to it; probably there isn't. But I have to exhaust some possibilities."

"And now you're demanding that I help you, out of the kindness of my heart?"

"I'm not demanding anything," I said, maintaining a calmness I was far from feeling. Frankly, all I wanted to do with this broad was to take that big wad of gum out of her mouth and... But I merely went on: "I'm asking you. As a favor. To me, to my friend Arthur Vance, and to your friend Gene Merriwether."

That shut her up for a bit.

Finally, she rolled her eyes and gave us both a put-upon grimace. "All right, you guys. Just because I'm so sweet."

Even Gene could tell that she was mocking him.

"Exactly how are you going to fit into this little scheme, Scintilla?" she went on.

"Well, if it's all right with you"—I included both Marge and Gene in my gaze—"I'd like to pose as a photographer. I won't say much—maybe nothing—but I'll just be there to take in everything that's said. How's that?"

"Sure!" Gene said before Marge could utter the protest she was no doubt preparing. "I'll check with Dan O'Connell—I'm sure he has a professional-looking camera he can lend you." He had all the enthusiasm of a schoolboy about to play a prank on the principal. Too bad some of that wasn't rubbing off on Marge.

But I guess she was a good girl in spite of her tough exterior. She called the Greenways and made an appointment for the next day.

The brownstone at 25 West 10th Street was an exquisite five-story brick structure just off Fifth Avenue—still soaked in the atmosphere of the Henry James–Edith Wharton milieu that, only a generation or so later, seemed as archaic and out of place in this Depression as the thatched hut of an African bushman. Before I had even met any of the Greenways I could tell that they belonged to that ever-dwindling class of old New Yorkers who were proud of never having lived north of 14th Street. I was not surprised when our summons was answered by a butler dressed in his penguin suit, who led us into a surprisingly ample foyer illuminated by a chandelier that still used candles. I almost expected to hear a Mozart string quartet playing in the background.

We were led into the drawing room, where a woman was seated on a Louis XV sofa with her back to us. She must have heard us come in, for she rose with alacrity, walked around the sofa, and faced us. I had my first look at Mrs. Elena Greenway.

She was tall, willowy, and with the deepest, richest black hair I had ever seen—far different from the corn-silk blonde of Katharine Vance. Her face was exceptionally fine—high cheekbones, delicate nose, lips just full enough to be sensuous without being vulgar, gentle but penetrating green eyes. She looked much younger than her age, which must have been approaching thirty; and yet her bearing was that of a mature woman entirely at home with herself and her circumstances. My heart skipped a beat when I saw her.

If Katharine Vance was anything like this, then I was no longer surprised that Arthur was desperate to get her back, even from the grave.

With a soft smile she greeted us as if we were old friends. "How do you do, Miss Schaeffer! So good to see you again." And, turning to me: "And you, Mr. O'Connell?" I had adopted the pseudonym of the camera's owner, with his permission. "What a heavy camera you have! I'm so pleased at your interest in me."

Her speech had a distinct trace of an Italian accent, although perhaps a little less than I had been led to expect.

Marge Schaeffer took control at once. In spite of the gruff boorishness she seemed to enjoy displaying at her office, she was in total command of the situation. She had not brought her chewing gum this time.

"Mrs. Greenway, it's so good of you to see us. Please pay no attention to Mr. O'Connell—just let him do his work and we'll do ours."

I ambled about, trying to look professional. I actually intended to take some pictures with this cumbersome device; they might come in handy. Meanwhile I made sure to keep my eyes and ears open.

Marge, her notepad on her lap, began: "Now let's just review some facts. You had come here in January of 1932 from Italy?"

"Yes, from Cattolica. Do you know it? A charming little beach resort on the Adriatic. A lovely town! I have such wonderful memories of it...although, of course, you know about my parents...."

"Well, honestly, I don't, Mrs. Greenway," Marge said.

I was looking at Elena through the camera lens. Her face would have had great difficulty being anything but beautiful, but it was now furrowed with pain.

"My parents...oh, they were such wonderful people! They died suddenly. Their boat capsized.... But, please, I don't wish to talk of them! It has been very hard for me...."

"Of course, Mrs. Greenway," Marge said with just the right amount of sympathetic concern. "I don't wish to upset you. But I wonder if you could tell us something of your youth and upbringing?"

I had coached Marge to make inquiries regarding Elena's background.

Mrs. Greenway responded promptly: "Oh, I had a lovely childhood! There is so much to tell...so much! My little girlfriends—and boyfriends, too, a little later!"—a girlish giggle—"all under that warm Italian sun! Oh, you have nothing like it here...except maybe in Florida or California."

Marge was sharp, and remembered my instructions. "Oh, have you been to California?"

"No, no," Mrs. Greenway said quickly—too quickly? "I just assume that your California and Florida might be like my Italy in that way...."

Very suave.

Marge continued: "So tell us, please, a bit more about your growing up in Italy. What schools did you go to?"

"Oh, there were several—you know they do not exactly correspond with your...how do you say, 'elementary' and 'high school'? Our schools were quite small, but we had wonderful teachers—wonderful! For a while I went to a school run by nuns—do you know I wished to be a nun once?" She laughed musically. "Oh, I knew so little of the world! But that dream passed quickly...very quickly!" Another laugh.

"Did you go to college?" Marge asked.

"Oh, yes—the *università* at Padua. I did not wish to go to Rome—Rome such a big city, you know. I was so scared! Ah, but Padua is a lovely little place—just right for me!" She beamed at us.

"And so you came here early in 1932?" Marge said.

"Yes...on that big boat, *Rè di Ponto*. It was the biggest journey I had ever taken, and I was so afraid—all by myself! But Mr. Greenway was very kind, taking me in like that. Ah, he has the Italian sense of *famiglia!* A wonderful man.... And so we fell in love, and—how do you say?—we live happily ever after!"

There was much more of this kind of thing, but that is all I can endure to write down. I don't wish to suggest that Mrs. Greenway was quite as brainless and schoolgirlish as the above might sound; in fact, I distinctly got the impression that she was "talking down" to us—we were mere newspaper reporters, after all—and giving us what she thought we and our readers wanted. Behind her inane words I could sense something peculiar—as if she were laughing at us. No, not that exactly: perhaps more as if she was simplifying a far more complex story that she didn't think we could understand.

Anyway, I quickly reached one conclusion: Either the former Miss Elena Cavalieri was the real thing—really was Elena Cavalieri, now Mrs. Harry Greenway—or had been exceptionally well coached. She had everything down pat. No hesitation, no confusion, no fumbling for words.

Was it too pat? Was it all a prepared speech? How could she know in advance what we had wanted to ask? Perhaps she had given interviews of this kind before—although Marge didn't know of any.

We stayed no longer than forty minutes; there didn't seem much point. On the cab ride back to the *Herald-Tribune* office, Marge asked:

"So, Scintilla, did you find what you were looking for?"

"Well, Miss Schaeffer, I'm not sure exactly what it is that I am looking for. But this was of some help. I think I remember most of what Mrs. Greenway said, but perhaps I could trouble you to get me a copy of your notes."

"I'll get them to you right away. And I wonder"—a bit wistfully—"whether you could keep me posted on your progress."

She seemed a lot more friendly and cooperative now. Too bad the gum had returned to its customary place in her mouth.

She looked a lot better without it.

CHAPTER FOURTEEN

I had been an idiot.

I've said that a good many of my successes in detection have resulted from identifying where and how my suspects have committed some act of stupidity, folly, or irrationality that betrayed them, leaving some vital clue that diligent research can follow up. I hadn't yet found that clue in the Removal Company case, but I was confident that it would come.

But there have also been some occasions—more, perhaps, than I care to admit—when I myself have ventured into incompetence or mere carelessness. This was one of those times.

Arthur Vance had long ago given me his wife's notebook or diary; but an initial glance at it had not impressed me. It seemed like the usual array of schoolgirlish confessions—the desperately cherished repository of the unremarkable secrets of a small and insignificant life. To a great degree it was just that; maybe it had some value as a "human document," but that was none of my concern.

Well, it had a bit more than that. It took some careful reading, but one fact of towering importance was lurking there if only you looked hard enough.

It all lay in a few diary entries of early December 1929, only a few weeks after the death of Katharine's father. The household was being broken up: the Hawleys had no more money left except the property they owned, and this was being sold in order to generate some income for Katharine and her mother to live on. What we find is this:

December 3. I've just learned that all the servants will have to go—we'll try to keep Soames, but that's probably all. Oh, God, can things get any worse? How ashamed and humiliated I feel! What will I do without my María?

Only a few days later there is this:

December 6. Everyone's concerned about how poorly I feel. That's sweet of them, but I think I'm past help now. I just wish the earth would swallow me up! That would be the best thing that could happen to me.

And then, the next day:

December 7. I wish everyone would stop hounding me! They all want me to see a psychiatrist, or even check myself into a hospital. Oh, I'll never do that!—never, never! Well, maybe I'll take up María's suggestion and see that Dr. Grabhorn. But I think it's a waste of money—and we certainly don't have very much of that now.

"I think I'll take up María's suggestion...." That one sentence sent me back to Los Angeles.

* * * * * * *

I walked into police headquarters in Pasadena pretty early on the morning after I arrived. By chance I met Detective Gulliver Crane in the hallway. He recognized me, accosted me with a grunt, and said:

"Say, Scintilla, you still think your man is innocent?"

"I do." I really didn't want to talk with him right now—I wanted to see Vance and ask what he knew about his wife's former maid.

"You want to see the police report? It's pretty much done. We've already booked Vance for second-degree murder."

"Only second-degree?" I said. "That's generous of you."

Crane shrugged magnanimously. "Well, I'm willing to believe it wasn't premeditated. Heat of the moment, you know? Vance seems a bit on the agitated side, no?"

"Yes." I wished this guy would shut up.

But Gulliver wasn't about to quit. Grabbing my arm, he said: "Come on, take a look. Maybe you New York boys don't think we know how to run a police investigation."

I didn't feel like nurturing Crane's inferiority complex, but I followed. Vance wasn't going anywhere.

Crane took me into his office and had me sit down in the chair in front of his desk, while he dropped himself heavily in his own chair. Pulling out a file from a side drawer, he shoved it in my direction.

"Here. Read it and weep."

Why was Crane so gleeful? Did he really get some kind of pleasure out of all this?

I decided to shake him up as best I could. "I don't suppose you've had any luck tracking down who made that anonymous phone call that brought you boys down to the Grabhorn—er, Greer place so fast?"

"No." By Crane's tone I could tell that he had made no effort to do so and considered it a waste of time even to bother trying.

I looked at the file. It was the usual stuff—photographs of the crime scene, coroner's report on Grabhorn/Greer, preliminary interrogation of Vance (not very informative), and suchlike. I flipped through it quickly, trying not to look at Crane's smug face.

Then one thing struck me. I pulled out a photograph—one of several of Vance.

"Hey, Crane, look at this."

He bent forward a little suspiciously, as if I were going to play an unpleasant magic trick on him.

"What is it?"

"Just look at this picture. It's of Vance's hands. Right?"

"Of course." Crane leaned back; the self-satisfied smirk had returned. "We wanted an airtight case, Scintilla. Not only did we test Vance's gun and bullet with the bullet that killed Greer—a perfect match, naturally—but we wanted to show that only Vance could have pulled the trigger."

"How do you prove that? Finger-prints?"

Crane actually chortled. "That's the easy part. Yes, of course, finger-prints: Vance's, and only Vance's, were on the gun. But we wanted to do more. Surely you know, Scintilla, that on almost any gun, and especially the large-caliber one Vance used, there are going to be powder marks on the hand that pulls the trigger. And that's exactly what you see there."

"So this"—I held up the picture—"was taken at the crime scene?"

"Oh, yes. Probably only minutes after the act, I'd say."

"Yes, maybe." I moved forward, placing the photo on his desk, facing him. "But there's something odd. Notice that there are only powder marks on Vance's fingers—not on the back of the hand. How exactly do you account for that?"

Crane peered down at the photo with the momentary thought that it might attack him. "Oh, come on, Scintilla, you're reaching...."

"But it's true, isn't it? What gives, Crane?"

Gulliver fumbled for words. "Well...maybe he was wearing gloves...."

It was my turn to smirk. "You'll have to do better than that. If he'd been wearing gloves, there wouldn't be any powder marks on his hand at all. And you didn't find any gloves on him or anywhere near him, did you?"

"No"—very quietly.

"Well, then."

"Wait a minute, shamus. You're trying to build up a case—or should I say you're trying to destroy our case—on something so slim as that? It won't work, Scintilla. No court in the world will follow you in that. You think that's enough for 'reasonable doubt'?"

"No," I said. "I think that's enough to prove that Vance is innocent of murder."

For a few seconds Crane appeared unable to comprehend what I had said. Then he exploded: *"What?"*

"Just calm down, man," I said. "And give me your gun."

This comment seemed to take him aback even more than its predecessor. He could literally not speak for several moments. Finally:

"What...what the devil do you want my gun for? You gonna blow my brains out—or yours?"

"Hardly," I said, chuckling politely at what I perceived—hoped—was a witticism. "Just give me the gun; and make sure to leave the safety on."

Like a man in a trance Crane did as he was told.

"Okay," I said, picking it up. "Now remember that Vance claimed that he had been struck by someone as soon as he came into the house, and woke up to find himself propped up on a wall in Greer's bedroom, the gun in his hand." I held up my hand to ward off the explosion I knew would come. "I know, Crane, I know—you don't believe any of that. But let's just go along with it for a moment, okay?"

I surveyed his office quickly. It was small and congested, but I guess it would do. "Here," I said, giving Crane back the gun, "take this and sit down on the floor over there—just prop yourself against those file cabinets."

Crane sputtered a bit more, but did as I said. His lumbering body didn't go down to the floor easily or lightly. A pained or irritated grunt escaped him as he hit the floor.

"All right. Now imagine that I am the fellow who coshed Vance. What do I do then? You see, I've already coshed Greer—that's how he got that wound on the back of his head, not by hitting his head on the mantelpiece after he'd been shot. It would have been easy to have rubbed the blood on the mantelpiece afterwards.

"So there you are. Vance is sitting up against one wall, Greer is propped against the wall of the fireplace. Both are unconscious. So what does the real assassin do?"

I bent down to where Crane was sitting. I picked up his hand, which was holding the gun. I placed my hand over his own—it now covered the entire back of his hand. I pulled the trigger, using Crane's own finger.

"That's it."

I got up a bit stiffly myself. My knees aren't what they used to be.

Crane was looking down at himself—at his hand, at his gun, and perhaps, in his mind's eye, at the collapse of his case.

He got up explosively, quicker than I thought possible for so stocky a man. "Goddammit, Scintilla! You're just too clever for your own good! Who's going to believe that? This isn't some Sherlock Holmes story, man! It just won't fly."

But he didn't sound very sure of himself.

"But it might fly as a case of 'reasonable doubt,' don't you think?"

He glared at me for an instant, then threw his gun on his desk. "Maybe," is all he could bring himself to say. For a moment he kept his back to me; then he wheeled around and said:

"So who *is* the gunman, Scintilla? You got *him* up your sleeve, too?"

"No," I said. "I have some ideas on that, but nothing definite to go on. Frankly, this murder case is only part of a bigger picture—there's other things I have to do. But you might query Greer's neighbors to see if they saw some other man fleeing from the place about the time of the murder. And while you're at it"—I couldn't resist this—"you'd better ask which one of them called the police.

"I think you'll find that none of them did."

With that, I left him.

CHAPTER FIFTEEN

"Scintilla!" Vance burst out when he saw me coming toward his cell. "What are you doing here? Did you find out something about Elena Cavalieri?"

"Not yet," I said. "But I may be on to something else." I looked him in the face. "Do you happen to know the last name of your wife's maid—the maid she had before she married you?"

"Katharine's *maid?*" he exploded. "How on earth should I know anything about her maid? And who cares about her maid anyway?"

"Vance, you little fool." I wanted to throttle him just then. "That maid was the one who tipped your wife off to Dr. Grabhorn."

Vance was thunderstruck. It actually shut him up for several moments.

"Her maid.... Her *maid!*" The thing seemed beyond his comprehension. "What on earth...? What's going on, Scintilla?"

"I don't know—yet. Maybe it was dumb luck—although I very much doubt it."

"You think"—Vance was all eagerness again, scarcely realizing that he himself was still under indictment for murder—"you think that this maid and Grabhorn were in cahoots, or something?"

"The maid, Grabhorn, Sanderson—maybe all of them are in it together. With the...er, hefty fees that Sanderson was charging for his 'services,' he could afford to hire a whole army of underlings, side-kicks, and drudges of various sorts."

"I *knew* it, Scintilla! I knew it! I knew there was something funny about this whole business.... Forget about this maid: you have to go back to New York and take my wife away from this Greenway fellow...."

I was having trouble following his train of thought. "Vance, what are you talking about? I'm not taking anybody away from anyone. We're not at that stage yet, and may never be. One thing at a time...."

"Goddammit, Scintilla," Vance roared, almost dancing with rage, "don't you see that I'm right in everything I've said? What's the—"

"No!" I shot back, banging the bars of his cell in my own fury.

That brought both of us up short. We both took some deep breaths.

"Vance," I said, as quietly as I could, "get a grip on yourself. I know this situation has been difficult for you, but you have to stay calm. Running ahead of yourself and flying off the handle isn't going to get you anywhere.

"You don't seem to grasp that there are two separate phases of this whole matter. There's all the stuff leading up to your wife's going to the Removal Company, and then there's the stuff that may or may not have happened afterward. The two things may or may not have anything to do with each other.

"Don't you get it?" I said impatiently. "No matter what kind of system Sanderson had to get his 'clients'—no matter how many maids or psycho-analysts or whoever he had or has in his pay—his whole operation may still be on the up-and-up...he naturally has to act covertly, given what he's trying to do.

"Right now we're on the track of his channel of communication. Beyond that, we don't have *anything*. We have *no* suggestion that he's not what he says he is—an assister in suicide—and on top of that, I've found *no* evidence that this Elena Cavalieri woman is not who she says she is.

"Arthur," I said, gently, "you still need to face the possibility—or even the probability—that your wife is dead."

Vance's face twisted up in a grimace of pain and grief. I was about as sorry for him as I had ever been. It's been a long time since I loved a woman, but I still knew how it felt.

But I'll say this for Arthur Vance: he wasn't a quitter. After a few moments he became galvanized again, spinning around to face me.

"But what about Grabhorn's murder, Scintilla? What about that?"

"What about it? I'm convinced now that you didn't do it"—that made him jolt backward in surprise—"but we don't know where it fits in yet. We don't have much to go on as far as that's concerned, so I'm not going to pursue it for a while."

"But...but what's going to happen to me?" Vance said worriedly. "Are they going to...am I going to be put on trial? God, that would be awful to my family...."

"Rest easy, Vance. I talked with Detective Crane; I think he sees things a little differently now. You're not in the clear yet, but I'm confident the charges against you will be dropped eventually. At least you may now be able to get out on bail."

"You can count on that," Vance said with a peculiar grimness. I wasn't sure what he meant.

"Look, Vance, that's not the point right now. Let's get back to this maid. It's important. If you don't remember her full name, do you know anyone who does? Your mother?"

"No," Vance said ruminatively, "I don't think so.... Your only chance may be with Mrs. Hawley—you know, Katharine's mother. I'm *sure* she knows!"

"Yes," I said, "that seems likely. But I'm not acquainted with her. Do you think your mother can be prevailed upon to make the inquiry?"

"Of course," Vance said. We could have been talking about setting up a bridge game. "She'll be happy to. And, Scintilla, you were planning to stay with us while you're here, weren't you?"

"I hadn't expected it, but that's nice of you."

We shook hands and I left.

* * * * * * *

From Mrs. Hawley, via Mrs. Vance, I found that the elusive maid was one María Rivera. That was not helpful. I didn't even want to contemplate how many María Riveras there were in southern California.

Well, there was nothing to do but begin the hunt. I had had Mrs. Vance ask where María had come from, and Mrs. Hawley gave the expected answer—some employment agency for domestic servants, she couldn't remember which. I pulled out the Los Angeles yellow pages, and found to my astonishment that there were as many as seven such establishments, with perhaps several others who didn't specialize in domestics but who might have handled them. I knew that my hunt would be long and tedious. At least Mrs. Vance was not a stickler about how much gasoline or tire rubber I used up.

And I used up quite a bit of it. The first four employment agencies were eliminated, although at considerable effort. One of them had three different María Riveras, but none of them seemed to be the woman I was after. I began to wonder whether the maid had used a fictitious name, but dismissed the thought as unlikely: it would have caused her too many complications. Grabhorn/Greer had found that out when he did his name-switching act.

The fifth place rung the bell. This establishment prided itself on catering to the refined needs of the upper classes. María Rivera had registered with the agency as far back as 1923, having come up from Mexico. At that time she had given her age as eighteen. She had been taken on, so I was told by the agency's manager, because she herself was unusual for foreign domestics: spoke English perfectly, although with an accent, and had a thorough knowledge of clothing, cosmetics, even hairdressing—a perfect maid for the lady who wished to look her best. María's employment record was as follows:

> September 1923–May 1925: Miss Harriet Lindsay, 9769 South Van Ness Avenue, Inglewood.
> June 1925–February 1927: Mrs. Edgar Grantham, 6214 San Vicente Boulevard, Santa Monica.
> March 1927–December 1929: Miss Katharine Hawley, 416 Huntington Drive, San Marino.
> January 1930–September 1931: Miss Priscilla James, 1324 North Mar Vista Avenue, Pasadena.
> November 1931–November 1932: Mrs. Henry Gold, 2921 East Slauson Avenue, Huntington Park.

It was an impressive list, judging by the addresses alone. María had not come cheap, evidently. But a few things puzzled me. I turned to the manager—a Mr. John Coryell—and said:

"It seems to me that she had a lot of different positions—or rather, positions at a lot of different households. Scarcely more than a year at some places. Isn't that a bit odd?"

Coryell was suave and ingratiating. "Well, Mr. Scintilla, one can never tell about the predilections of these upper-class ladies. The matter of a personal maid is a very sensitive one, as you can imagine. In no case was María dismissed for cause, and none of these ladies had anything but the highest praise for her work. As you can see, she was hired almost immediately to her next position after she had left the previous one. She was much in demand."

I let that go; I didn't know much about maids, or the women who used them.

"Where is María now?" I asked. "What happened to her when she left this stint last November?"

Coryell winced at the word "stint"—perhaps it was a little too vulgar for him—but was otherwise unflappable. "Oh, María said she had to return to her family in Mexico. I was sorry to lose her...."

"You mean she came here in 1923 alone?—at the age of eighteen? There was no family here with her?"

"Ah, Mr. Scintilla, María was very capable of looking after herself."

I was getting to dislike Coryell's wide smile and his perfect teeth. "So there's no family member here I can talk to about María? And you don't know where she now is?"

Coryell felt only my last question was worth the bother of answering. "Mexico is a large country, Mr. Scintilla."

I had by now finished copying down the addresses of the ladies with whom María had worked. As I did so, Mr. Coryell looked at me a bit apprehensively.

"I'm aware, sir," he said, "that you have your investigations to pursue. But I do trust that you will not bother these ladies unduly...."

"Why?" I said sharply. "What's it to you?"

Coryell was taken aback by the remark, but regained his composure instantly. "Nothing at all, Mr. Scintilla, nothing at all. But surely you know that an agency like mine has a reputation to protect...."

"Don't worry," I said, "I won't mention your company, or say where I got these addresses from."

Coryell was all smiles again. "You're very kind, Mr. Scintilla."

I wasted as few additional words with him as possible and left the place.

* * * * * * *

María was—if Coryell was telling the truth—not an easy pigeon to track down; but I began to think that she was the least of my concerns. What I really wanted to know was what—if anything—had happened to the various women who had employed her. If they were all part of Los Angeles high society, then I figured that one good place to start would be close to home—Mrs. Henry Vance.

She peered at my list of names with interest and attention. "Priscilla...I hadn't any idea she had hired María after the Hawleys had dismissed her.... Most remarkable." Her brow was furrowed with a mixture of concern and puzzlement.

"Priscilla James?" I said. "Do you know her?"

"Well, yes, of course," Mrs. Vance said. "Or, rather, we did. She... well, she left town rather abruptly, I thought."

A chill went through me.

"When was that?" I asked.

"Oh, only a few months ago. It was all a bit odd. She just up and left one day—leaving behind a very nice home and all her things.... Then a little later one of our friends, the Copleys, got a strange letter from her saying that she had fallen in love with a Frenchman and was now living in Lyons! It was quite extraordinary. And that's the last we ever heard from her."

As I was mulling that over, I asked Mrs. Vance: "Do you know any of the other names on that list?"

She peered at the list again, as if it were a kind of school examination. "Well, yes...Frances Grantham—a lovely person—and Helen Gold. Why, I just saw her a few weeks ago."

"Then she's still alive?" I blurted out.

Mrs. Vance looked at me with astonishment. "Oh, dear me, yes! Whatever can you be thinking?"

"Sorry...I didn't mean that. And Mrs. Grantham?"

"Well," said Mrs. Vance, "I haven't seen her in some months—she's really not part of our set, you see—but I imagine she is in the land of the living!" She considered that a great witticism.

"Thank you, Mrs. Vance."

I left the room, shaking a bit. Something was very wrong here. Who was this Priscilla James—and what had happened to her? I got to work on the case immediately.

* * * * * * *

Results came quickly. Miss James's house in Pasadena had, I learned, been put up for sale—furnishings and all—and at the moment was being looked after by a caretaker. Miss James's lawyer, Marlon Wright, regularly received sums of money from a New York lawyer to cover the expenses. Wright was a bit puzzled by this arrangement, but he had received a handwritten letter from Miss James confirming them, so he had no option but to agree.

I took down the name of the New York lawyer.

I asked Wright only one more question: "Do you know whether Priscilla James was seeing a psychoanalyst at any time?"

Wright looked up at me in surprise. "Why, yes—how did you know?"

"Never mind that. Do you recall his name?"

"I do indeed—I paid his bills myself. It was one William Grabhorn. I believe he was on Wilshire Boulevard in Los Angeles. Shall I find the address for you?" He began fishing among his papers.

"That won't be necessary," I said.

* * * * * * *

Thanks to Mrs. Vance, the Copleys were only too happy to be of help to me. I didn't mince matters, and asked them to show me the letter from Priscilla James telling of her supposed romance with the Frenchman.

They brought out the letter immediately. I think it tickled them to be part of a private investigation.

I took the letter out of its envelope. It said pretty much what Mrs. Vance had told me.

"Is this Priscilla James's handwriting?" I asked Mrs. Copley.

"Oh, yes," she said promptly, "there's no mistaking it."

I turned the letter over indecisively. This could be on the level, although it seemed mighty suspicious. As with María Rivera, it would be difficult, and probably unprofitable, to try to track down Priscilla James in France—if that was where she was. Anyway, that would be taking me a bit far afield of my original inquiry.

Then I looked down at the envelope. I myself rarely keep envelopes of letters I receive, but I was more than a little thankful that the Copleys had done so.

It was postmarked from New York.

CHAPTER SIXTEEN

When I got back to the Vance house, Arthur was there.

"What...?" I said. "How did you..."

Vance gave a self-satisfied smirk. "Scintilla, we have a good law-yer. And we have the money for bail. After what you told me this morning, I made it clear to my people that I was getting pretty tired of being cooped up in jail. So here I am."

"Very nice for you, I'm sure."

"I'm still under indictment, and I'm not supposed to leave the state, but I think those things will be taken care of pretty soon."

"I hope so."

Then, as if his own concerns were not of the faintest interest to him, he said: "Now tell me—did you find María?"

"No, but I found out plenty about her."

I told him what I had learned during the long day. Vance's eyes goggled as each bit of information slipped from my lips, and the Priscilla James matter caused him to utter a thunderous oath and begin pacing about the room. After that he merely muttered over and over, "My God...my God...."

"I doubt that it would be worth pursuing María Rivera's other em-ployers," I said. "Some of them seem to be alive, but we have at least one other instance where she is likely to have referred a person to Grabhorn; and then he may—I repeat, Vance: *may*—have passed on Miss James to the Removal Company. But we don't know that yet."

"God, Scintilla, it's obvious! That's exactly what happened! This is becoming more hellish all the time...."

"Yes, maybe. But this really doesn't tell us a great deal more than we knew before. Okay, so Grabhorn has probably been caught in a lie—he may have referred more people than just your wife to Sanderson. But that's a minimal point: I'd been suspecting that all along."

Vance wheeled around. "But the maid! Don't you see? There was some sort of *pipeline* to the Removal Company! The maid—Grabhorn—and God knows who else—all these people were funneling likely clients to that devil Sanderson!"

"Vance, I hate to keep throwing cold water on you; but there's one problem in all this. We don't know that anyone was *forced* to go to Sanderson, or *forced* to commit suicide. It all seems voluntary—so far."

"Jesus, Scintilla, what more is it going to take?" Vance blazed at me.

"Look, man, we're still nowhere near figuring out what—if anything—happened to your wife. That's the rub. There may or may not be anything sinister in this 'pipeline,' as you call it. The crux, now, is to find out what happened *afterward.*"

Me and my big mouth.

"That's exactly right!" Vance almost shouted. "And that's where you come in!"

"What exactly do you mean by that?"

"Why, Elena Cavalieri, of course! You have to find out if her story checks out! Find out if she is who she says she is!"

"You mean...?"

"Yes, Scintilla. You're taking a trip to Italy."

* * * * * * *

I don't like boats. I don't like being off dry land. Somehow being in a plane is okay, because at least you're back on the ground in a few hours. But spending days or weeks on some immense body of water, with no land in sight, is not my idea of a good time.

I should have welcomed this trip to Italy, but I didn't. My grandmother, to be sure, was pure Italian, and had come to America in the 1870s, bringing her young daughter—my mother—with her. But the moment she settled in New York she was determined to "assimilate," and to have her offspring do likewise. My mother of course knew Italian, but spoke very little of it to my brother and me. I knew some words, but had forgotten the ability—if I had ever had it—to make coherent sentences. In my "native" land I would be as helpless as the most uncultured Midwestern tourist.

The boat, passing by the awe-inspiring crag known as Gibraltar, took six days to reach Marseilles. There, even though I would have preferred to make the rest of the journey on land, I had to switch for another boat, which took me to the port of Rimini, on the Adriatic. Once there I hired a guide (who would also serve as a translator), and also an unbelievably rickety contraption that I was soberly informed was an automobile.

The ten-mile drive from Rimini to Cattolica, along the coast road, was uneventful. If I had been less preoccupied—or less incensed with Arthur Vance for sending me on this wild goose chase—I might have appreciated the breathtaking vista of the Adriatic on our right, and the lush, rolling farmland on our left. I was not surprised that Mrs. Elena Greenway had compared her native region to California or Florida: there was a crispness in the air, a sharp, penetrating quality to the sunlight, a heat that seemed to radiate gently from the very earth, that brought the subtropics to mind. It may only have been late March, but it seemed as if summer was already in full flower.

Cattolica was exactly what Mrs. Greenway had said it was: a beach resort—the Italian equivalent of Miami Beach. The main street, almost facing the shore, was lined with hotels, and even in this off-season they seemed fairly well filled—not with foreign tourists, but with Italians. This was the place where the locals went: to loaf on the beach, to get away from mundane reality, perhaps to pretend desperately that they were really in Nice or Monaco.

I scarcely knew how or where to start my inquiries. I was pretty well acquainted with how American government—municipal, state, and federal—worked, but had not the faintest idea of their Italian equivalents. Also, it wasn't likely that my various credentials—genuine, false, or fudged—would open many doors for me. My excitable Italian guide didn't let me sit still for a moment, but took me directly to the town hall. It was as good a place as any to start.

I first tried an office where visas were issued. If Elena Cavalieri had come to the United States in early 1932, she had to have had a visa. But I was informed by the military-looking clerk that I would not be permitted to look at the visas issued during the last ten years—or, really, at any time.

How about phone books for the last couple of years? Another clerk informed me that none were issued, except a list of phone numbers of local businesses. The town was mighty small, and apparently everyone knew everyone else. Only those businesses catering to outside tourists could be easily found.

I went through the motions of asking about city directories, but was met with a look of complete bewilderment on the face of a third clerk.

I was not doing so well.

But if this small town was so tightly knit, one would imagine that the Cavalieris had been well known to their neighbors. But who *were* their neighbors? I couldn't knock on every door in the town and hope that someone knew them. The place wasn't *that* small.

It was my guide who came up with the brainstorm. Cattolica, it appeared, had only six Catholic churches. The Cavalieris would surely be—or have been—on the rolls of one of them. A detail like that would never have occurred to me. I guess there is a downside to being an agnostic.

And so began the rather frenetic canvassing of the churches. They were all small, and if I had been a student of architecture I could have found much interest in them. But I wasn't—or didn't want to be at the moment—and so my guide and I pressed on efficiently.

Once again, as with those employment agencies in Los Angeles, it took several misses before we hit upon the right one. But we did in the end. The chiesa di San Antonio was the place, and its priest distinctly remembered the Cavalieris. Wonderful people, he said; what a horrible tragedy to befall them. Mysterious are the ways of God. And so on.

At the moment all I wanted was their home address, so I urged the guide to get that information out of the priest. The guide pressed the point as tactfully as he could, using abundant hand gestures, and finally the priest led us back into his study and opened an enormous book.

Much flipping of pages at the beginning, and then this entry:

Cavalieri, Ettore e Sophia. 23, Via dei Principi. Elena, figlia. Mor. 21 Agosto 1931.

That third sentence had been added at a later time, the fourth at a still later time.

I almost dragged my guide back to the car. "Let's find the Via dei Principi. Right now."

The priest had offered minimal directions, pointing vaguely to the southwest. Still, it didn't take long to find—the street was quite small and terminated in a dead end.

Number 23 was almost the last house on the right. Incredibly, it was apparently still vacant: no one had occupied it in the year and a half since the Cavalieris had died and their only daughter left for America. I took a picture of the place with a small camera I had brought with me, but beyond that we weren't going to get much out of it. We decided to go to the nearest neighbor, directly to the right.

Our summons was answered by a middle-aged lady in loose-fitting clothing and a bandanna around her head. I had the guide get right to point.

"Ask her if she remembers the Cavalieris."

The moment he did so, the woman almost burst into tears, covering her mouth with her hands and goggling her eyes out of their sockets. She then began speaking extremely fast in Italian—so fast that even my guide had trouble keeping up with her.

"What's she saying?" I snapped. "What's going on? What is she telling you?"

"Wait, wait...," the guide said irresolutely, trying simultaneously to address me in English and the woman in Italian. Eventually he gained control of the situation, but could still only speak in fragments:

"Yes, yes...Cavalieris, nice people...wonderful...so kind...horrible thing to happen...boat capsized in the Adriatic one day...nobody could reach them fast enough, and they were trapped underneath...house thought to have 'bad luck,' so nobody use it...."

"Look, guy, this isn't helping. I knew all that. What about the daughter? What happened to Elena?"

The guide repeated my queries, but they only sent the woman into further lamentations. The guide tried to interpret as best he could:

"Yes, Elena...lovely girl...tall, slim, beautiful...like a queen...poor thing...."

I was almost consumed with rage and frustration. "Man, can't you get her to tell you what *happened* to Elena? When did she leave for America?"

But when the guide repeated my question, the woman almost gave a shriek and then slammed the door.

"What the...?" I said. "What is going on? Is she crazy?"

The guide merely shrugged sheepishly, as if apologizing for his country.

"This is absurd," I said heatedly. "Let's go back and see if that priest knows anything more."

So we drove back to the chiesa di San Antonio. We had come from a different direction, and so I noticed something I hadn't seen before—the surprisingly extensive cemetery abutting the church.

"Wait a minute," I said to the guide as he was almost flying by the cemetery. We pulled up with a jerk that almost thrust me through the windshield. With a glare of hostility at the guide I heaved myself out of the car.

Many of the tombstones were quite old, so I knew they wouldn't be of any use. After going about the cemetery almost in a circle I finally found some tolerably recent burial plots. In a few minutes I had located two still shining marble headstones placed in close juxtaposition:

ETTORE CAVALIERI   SOPHIA CAVALIERI

14 Aprile 1880   6 Decembre 1884
21 Agosto 1931   21 Agosto 1931

Well, that was something. I stepped back in order to get both of them in the photograph I wanted to take; but as I did so, I tripped backwards over another grave I had not seen before. It was new, but already nearly covered in tall grass.

Irritated, I tugged away some of the grass. What I saw was this:

ELENA CAVALIERI
16 Gennaio 1907
21 Agosto 1931

CHAPTER SEVENTEEN

Finally I had something. Finally I had come up with some definite clue that would allow me to say: "Something is not right here." This was something that the perpetrator—whoever he was—had over-looked, disregarded, or didn't believe would be noticed.

And yet, I wasn't sure exactly *what* it was that I had.

Elena Cavalieri had died with her parents in that boating accident—or had she? Who was in that grave that bore her name? Was there anyone there? Could that headstone be resting over an empty coffin, or undisturbed earth? What, really, was going on here? And who was responsible? Was the culprit really the shadowy Dr. Sanderson, or was it Grabhorn, or even Vance himself? Or was it some other party altogether? There were still too many missing pieces, too many places where inference had to take the place of evidence. The net was tightening, but it hadn't caught a fish yet.

I had to think through the matter systematically—and I had plenty of time to do that on the long boat ride back to New York. What I now knew, with tolerable certainty, was this:

There really had been some sort of "suicide pipeline" involving Grabhorn, the maid María Rivera, and Sanderson—and perhaps many others. Was Sanderson really behind it? The odds were good that he was.

Elena Cavalieri—the original Elena Cavalieri—was probably dead. When I returned to Rimini I checked that city's leading paper for the period in question and found a brief report on the accident, and it listed three fatalities, not just two. So the woman posing as Elena Cavalieri—now Mrs. Harry Greenway—was not who she said she was.

And yet, she was pretty convincing, at least superficially: she could recall her youth and adolescence in the village, knew what had happened to her parents, and had an account of her voyage here that was verifiable—as that Ellis Island immigration record proved.

So who was she? Was she really Katharine Vance? If so, how did she take on the personality of Elena Cavalieri?

I realized that the true crux of the matter was this:

What really happened to Dr. Sanderson's "clients" in that bizarre office of the Removal Company?

That was now the heart of the case, and that was what I had to devote all my attention to investigating when I came home.

But events forced me to take a different turn.

* * * * * * *

I had returned to New York late on the evening of March 31. Exhausted, I went to bed immediately. Numerous errands—not the least of which was the rapid development of those photographs I had taken in Italy—occupied much of the next day, and I didn't get back into my office until late in the afternoon.

I had scarcely taken off my hat when the phone rang.

"Scintilla," I said.

"Thank God you're back!"

It was Vance. I had written him about my expected date of arrival, but had not told him what I had found in Italy.

"Vance, is that you?" I said. "Where are you calling from?"

There was a curious silence on the other end.

"I can't tell you that, Scintilla.... Listen, you have to help me...."

What new scrape had this bird gotten himself into? I thought.

"What's the matter? Where are you? Why are you talking so funny?"

"Listen, Scintilla...I've— You see...."

"Christ, man, get it out!" I was rapidly losing patience.

Then Vance said: "Is this phone tapped?"

I closed my eyes for a moment. "Vance, what is this? What are you trying to pull?"

"Just answer me!" He sounded harried, desperate—almost out of control. "Please...*is your phone tapped?*"

"How the hell should I know?" I thundered. "Not that I know of...."

"Well," Vance said in a kind of conspiratorial whisper, "we have to assume that it might be. We have to meet, Scintilla."

"And how do you propose to do that?" I wasn't whispering. "You want me to fly across the country yet again?"

"I'm not in San Marino...I—I'm in New York."

"You're what?" I almost shouted. "Vance, you're still under indictment—you're not supposed to leave California."

"I know that—that's not important now...."

"Not important! I don't think you quite grasp—"

He cut me off. "Scintilla, listen to me! I've kidnapped Elena Greenway."

There was a silence. I could feel the blood rushing through my temples, hear my heart pounding. For a fleeting moment I thought I heard Vance's as well.

"You crazy fool!" I exploded. "What...how...?" I was spluttering with rage and bafflement.

"Look, Scintilla, we have to get together!" Vance said. "You know where I said I was staying when I first came to you? Do you remember?"

"Yes," I said quietly.

"Meet me there. Please—as fast as you can."

I hung up without saying anything more. Within a minute I had left the office and was making my way to 144 East 62nd Street.

* * * * * * *

It was Vance's uncle's place, I knew. The building was a four-story brick townhouse off Lexington Avenue, with entrance directly facing the sidewalk and large, arched windows on the second story. I had little doubt that Vance's uncle owned the entire place.

My brain was in a whirl. I felt both foolish and dazed as I rang the bell, as if I were coming to late afternoon tea. Within seconds I could see a head peering up through the panes set high in the door; then the door opened quickly.

It wasn't who I expected to see. I was met by Gene Merriwether.

"What on earth are you—?" I started.

"Never mind that," Merriwether whispered as he barely allowed me enough leeway to enter. "Just come on up."

I was in a narrow lobby with a staircase on the right. I mounted it. At the top I encountered a set of double doors, closed and—as I learned when I tried the knob—locked.

"Vance, are you in there?" I said sharply. "It's Scintilla; let me in."

The doors flung open and Vance stood there. He grabbed my lapel and saying, "Jesus, Scintilla, keep your voice down!" thrust me in, almost closing the double doors on Merriwether, who had marched up right behind me.

I stood facing a man who had undergone the effects of a prolonged rush of adrenalin: haggard, hair tousled, eyes glazed, sweat beading his forehead and upper lip, breathing stertorously, and seemingly ready to collapse of nervous exhaustion at any moment.

But that wasn't all I took in as I entered the large, tastefully furnished room. On a sofa sat—again to my surprise—Marge Schaeffer. On a wooden chair, evidently taken from the dining room table, sat Elena Greenway. She was disheveled, frightened, and bewildered; her hands were tied behind her, and her ankles were tied to the legs of the chair.

"For God's sake, Vance!" I shouted. "Untie that woman! Have you gone absolutely mad? What the bloody hell is the meaning of all this?"

Vance was slow to respond, so Elena filled in the silence. "Oh, thank the Lord!" she said in her Italian accent. "Mr. O'Connell...maybe that is not your real name...please, sir, you must help me! Please let me go back to my husband! He'll pay you anything you want! This madman—"

That got Vance going. "*I'm* your husband, Katharine! *I* am! You're my wife!"

Elena winced and tried as far as possible to move away from him.

She didn't get very far.

I felt like throttling everyone in sight, but tried to regain composure.

"Vance," I said softly, "please tell me what is going on. What have you done?—and why? First, how did you get out of California?"

Vance actually smirked at the question. "Scintilla, do you really think I was going to stay cooped up in my house doing nothing? Getting out was the easiest part. There was no surveillance on me: the police know me and my family, and I'll go back anytime they want. All I did was to hire a private plane to take me to Phoenix, and from there I just stepped on Pan Am 647 and came here."

I paused in thought. Looking around at each occupant of the place—the frazzled Vance, the terrified Elena, the sheepish Merriwether, and the strangely demure Marge—I turned my attention back to Vance and said, in a quiet but threatening voice:

"You deliberately sent me to Italy to get me out of the way, didn't you?"

In rage I lunged at him, grabbing him by the collar. *"Didn't you?"*

Vance was taken aback; didn't know what to do. Merriwether came to his aid and tried to pull me off. But I wasn't letting go.

"Scintilla," Vance said in a choking voice, "you got it all wrong! That wasn't it at all! I mean, you wrote you found something in Italy, didn't you? I just got tired of doing nothing.... I was going mad, Scintilla!"

I let him go, grudgingly. "Well, you've certainly done that."

Marge chimed in: "Please, Mr. Scintilla, take it easy on him. He's been through a lot...."

"*He* has!" I exploded. "What about her?"—pointing to Elena.

Marge winced, but said nothing.

"Vance," I resumed, "tell me the meaning of this. First of all, how the hell did you pull it off? Surely you didn't just walk into the Greenway home and take her away."

Vance chuckled. "Well, Scintilla, that's exactly what I did! The police still have my gun, so I went to Chinatown, bought another one"—he gestured with incredible nonchalance at an immense revolver lying on the dining room table, something that might have come out of a cowboy movie—"and, yes, then *I just walked into the Greenway home and took her away!*"

He beamed at me in pride. I could not utter, so he continued:

"It was easy! Nobody there had any weapons—anyway, there was only that butler and Mr. Greenway. I just told Elena—er, Katharine—to pack a few things, and then I walked out.

"Now listen to this, Scintilla. That was three days ago. Since that time *the police have not been notified, and there has been nothing published in the papers about this kidnapping.* Doesn't that tell you something?"

He had something there. "Yes, it does—but I'm not sure what."

"Don't you see?" Vance almost shouted. "They're afraid! We have them on the run! They don't dare say anything to anyone, because the whole thing will unravel."

"Who exactly is 'they'?" I asked.

"Why," Vance said, a little uneasily, "Sanderson of course! And Greenway, too, probably—they're all in it. I'm sure of it!"

I let that pass. Vance could be right, or he could merely be getting paranoid.

All I said was: "So what happens now?"

There was complete silence for several moments. Vance looked around to his two compatriots—he didn't seem keen on looking at Elena—but found no answers there: they merely looked back at him inquiringly, and rather nervously.

"I'm not sure," Vance finally said, slowly. "We have to force their hand somehow...." He began to pace about, as if that might help his brain work.

"Vance," I said, tiredly, "you've made things a lot more difficult. I told you I'm on to something. You should have let me handle this. You've gotten yourself into deep trouble, and there may be no way to get you out of it."

Vance looked at me in wide-eyed desperation. "My God, Scintilla, you've got to help me! We're so close...aren't we? We have to do something...."

"The first thing we do," I said forcefully, "is to untie this woman." When no one moved, I shouted: *"Untie her! Now!"*

After a moment Marge Schaeffer leaped up and did as I had commanded. Both Vance and Merriwether momentarily thought of trying to stop her, but a glare from me brought them up short.

Marge freed Elena in moments—the knots had not been tied very tight. Nevertheless, Elena rubbed her wrists and ankles briskly, whimpering a little and still looking petrified.

I went up to her. "Can you get up, ma'am?" I said.

"Yes," she said in a small voice, "I think so."

"Scintilla, what are you doing?" Vance said in alarm.

"Butt out of this, Vance," I snapped back. I looked around at the several doors in the room. "Is there a place where this woman can lie down?"

Vance almost sprang to one of the doors, opening it wide. "Yes," he said, "my uncle's bedroom. He's away on a cruise—won't be back for several weeks."

"Fine." I led Elena to the room. When Vance made an effort to go in with me, I stopped him with a hand on his chest. "No, Vance."

He began to sputter. "What...what are you going to do with her?"

"I have to talk to her alone. I mean that—*alone*."

Reluctantly he let me close the door in his face.

I turned back to Elena Greenway, who was standing irresolute in the middle of the room. She looked a little less scared, but still apprehensive. Clearly I had not won her trust, and doubted that I ever would.

"Ma'am," I said, "maybe you'd just better rest for a while. Nothing is going to happen to you. You'll be all right. But just rest now."

I wasn't very good at this sort of thing, but it seemed to work: she mutely did as I said.

I think she may actually have slept for about half an hour. After that, with a little moan, she awoke, then almost sprang from the bed, looking terrified again.

I placed my hand gently on her arm. "It's all right. Take it easy, it's all right."

She slowly fell back on the bed.

I turned on the light. It was a bit too bright, and both of us squinted at the sudden illumination.

"Do you mind," I said, "if I ask you some questions?"

"No," she replied, still in that small voice.

"All right."

I had no idea how she would respond to what I was about to ask her, but I knew that her answers would be vital in solving this case.

I first took out a photo of the house where Elena Cavalieri had supposedly grown up, and placed it in her hand.

"Do you recognize that place?"

She looked puzzled, then almost angry. "No. No, I do not. What is it?"

She made as if to hand it back to me, but I gently pressed her to look at it again.

"Are you sure? Absolutely sure?"

"Yes, of course. I have not seen that place. Never!"

I took the picture back from her. "All right." I gave her a photo of the church of San Antonio. "How about this?"

She scarcely glanced at the picture. "No. I do not know this place either. Is this Italy? There are many churches in Italy!" She almost chuckled at her witticism.

There was something extremely strange going on here. Her responses were, in several ways, not what I had expected. If she was Elena Cavalieri, she would have recognized the photos instantly. If she were merely an actress who had been coached to pretend that she was Elena, then she should at least have made a pretense of recognizing the photos. But instead, she absolutely denied any recognition, and seemed entirely sincere and guileless in doing so.

I felt I had to go the distance.

"How about this?"

It was the photo of the graves of her parents.

"No...ah, yes! Oh, my God, my parents! Yes, yes, of course I know this!"

But she hadn't at first. Only when she saw the names on the tombstones did she claim any remembrance.

"Now about this."

It was the photo of Elena Cavalieri's gravestone.

For a moment she peered squintingly at the photograph. Then an instant of comprehension.

She shrieked, then fell in a dead faint.

* * * * * * *

The door burst open, and all three of the other occupants of the place rushed in. Vance looked at me ferociously, but I shrugged that off and told him to call his doctor and have him come here immediately. Looking sharply between me and the woman on the bed, he grudgingly followed my orders.

Dr. Williamson—Vance's uncle's personal doctor—came within fifteen minutes. He took one glance at the prostrate woman and flashed a look of utter bewilderment, almost of horror, at Vance and the rest of us. I think he had recognized someone.

A cold compress and gentle applications of smelling-salts did the trick. The woman's eyes fluttered, then opened wide.

Vance dashed to her side, took up her hand, and said, pleadingly: "Katharine...Katharine, is that you?"

She looked puzzled, but not at the man she was looking at.

"Arthur...Arthur, what am I doing here? Where am I?" There was no longer any Italian accent.

Vance's voice quivered. "You're safe, Katharine. Safe."

Katharine Vance had, after a fashion, come home.

CHAPTER EIGHTEEN

I was sitting at dinner with Marge Schaeffer. It wasn't Delmonico's, but it was a nice place.

The turmoil following Katharine Vance's "return" to herself would be difficult to imagine. I think Arthur wanted to let out a whoop of triumph, but out of consideration for his still shaken wife he restrained himself, giving me merely a silent glance of satisfaction. I didn't begrudge him his victory: he had been proven right.

And yet—as I told him after pulling him away from the others—our problems were far from over. Not only did we still need to figure out what exactly had happened to Katharine—and given her present condition, we weren't likely to know anytime soon, if at all—but we still needed to track down Dr. Sanderson, the presumable culprit behind all the incredible events of the past year and a half. Also, Katharine was still married—at least in the eyes of the law—to Harry Greenway, and it would require some mighty tall talking to establish that the marriage was bigamous.

But Sanderson was our man now. We had to get him. And as yet we hadn't even the faintest hope of doing so.

Katharine Vance, meanwhile, had been sedated, and Dr. Williamson quickly arranged to have several nurses provide round-the-clock care. She would be out of commission for a long time.

What exactly had happened to her? My immediate thought was some kind of hypnosis. She had been tutored to absorb the basic facts of Elena Cavalieri's life—had even been given an Italian accent. But there had been a flaw in the plan: she had merely been told that she had been born in Cattolica, and had never been taken there, or seen photographs of her own supposed home, or the gravesite of her parents. That's why she honestly didn't recognize the photos of these sites that I had shown her.

It was a bad slip-up. And it showed me that Sanderson was capable of making mistakes. Were there others?—others that would allow us to beard him in his lair?

My head was too full now—I could hardly think coherently. Marge Schaeffer took pity on me—said I'd better get something to eat, then take a long rest. When Vance made a motion to join us, Marge put her arm on his chest as I had done, saying:

"No, Arthur. He needs to get away from you for a while."

* * * * * * *

Marge was a good interviewer—but I'd known that before. Without being in the least obtrusive about it, she got me to say more about myself than I do to most people. It took a while, but she managed it.

"You play things pretty close to the vest, don't you, Joe?"

I shrugged. "I'm not sure I know what you mean."

"Oh, your likes, your dislikes, why you do what you do, what your goals and dreams are. Things like that."

I smiled wearily. "A good private investigator has to learn to button his lip—sometimes even to his clients."

"I'm not one of your clients." She smiled.

I smiled back. "No. You certainly aren't."

I devoted myself resolutely to the steak and French fried potatoes on my plate. Marge had been a bit less indulgent and had ordered a chef salad.

"Do you like what you do?" she said at last.

"Sure," I said. "It doesn't pay very well, but it seems to be what I do best. Do you like what you do?"

It was her turn to shrug. "I'm not so sure. Like Gene, I'd like to be something other than a society reporter. It's pretty limiting. And there are times when I want to give a good swift kick in the pants to the 'society people' I'm supposed to be fawning over."

She grinned from ear to ear. She was one of the few women who didn't look unattractive doing it.

I grinned back. "Lady, you haven't met some of my clients."

"Like Arthur?" she said, provocatively.

"Vance? No, not Vance. He's a good guy, basically. He stuck with his intuitions. It was an incredible long shot, and I understandably doubted him for a long time, but he was right. I'll give him that much.

"His problems are far from over; in some ways they're just beginning. But at least he has his wife back."

We both ate some more.

I got the impression that Marge was debating whether to say something. It appeared that my last remark had given her an opening, and she wasn't certain whether to take it or not. In the end she did:

"What about you, Joe? Any wife for you?"

"No."

I didn't mean to be brusque, but maybe it came off that way. Marge seemed hesitant to proceed, afraid that she'd offended me.

"I don't want to pry...."

"It's not that." I shook my head. "I don't see myself getting married. I don't think any woman would have me...."

Marge laughed. "Joe, that's an old line! Very old!"

"Okay, but it may still be true."

"Or maybe it's a shield."

"Maybe."

There was another silence. Then Marge reached over and placed her hand gently on mine. "Look, Joe, I don't mean anything by this. I was just curious—curious whether you have a place for women in your life."

"I did once." It's amazing to me how men—even those who play it close to the vest—jump at opportunities to lay bare their hearts to a woman. Do all men think of all women as potential replacements for their mother?

All Marge said was: "Yes...?"

It would have been awkward to have zipped my lip now, so I just let it out.

"It was years ago—I couldn't have been more than twenty-five, and I'd been a P.I. only a couple of years. Yes, it was a client. A very bad thing to get involved with a client—I knew that, of course, but I was a lot less in control of my emotions then than I am now.

"She was in an ugly divorce case, and I had to get some dope on her husband. She was so young—a few years younger than me—had married at a very early age, and realized pretty soon that it was a mistake. So did he, I guess, for he made no bones about fooling around. I had to do a lot of hand-patting—you know, letting her cry on my shoulder, that sort of thing. It was a tough situation for a man who hadn't had a girl since high school."

I looked off in the distance, hardly seeming to talk to anyone in particular.

"Yes, she was pretty, but more than that, she was the most *feminine* woman I've ever met—every word, every gesture of hers was so emphatically proclaimed her sex, and without the least suggestion of a 'come-on' or anything like that. And she was still so naïve—hard to believe she'd been married for five years.

"Well, after her divorce went through we naturally talked about marriage. Of course, we didn't want to rush into anything, given her bad experience, but it seemed clear to us that we had a future.

"Then things just fell apart. She hated the city, wanted to move upstate. I knew that my life, my career, were here—and I loved the pace, the throb of New York. I couldn't go anywhere else—I'd have to give up my job altogether and do something entirely different. We had bitter fights—all the more baffling to us because we still seemed to love each other so much. I was infuriated that she couldn't see things my way, and I know she felt the same. But maybe there really was no misunderstanding: we both knew what the stakes were. We knew that one of us would have to give in, yield to the other. And neither of us was willing to do that.

"And yet, toward the end I offered to do just that—throw up my job and live with her wherever she wanted. It was irrational, of course—and she knew it. She knew that if I did that, we might be happy for a while, but then I would come to hate her for what she had made me do. She loved me enough not to want that.

"So we just went our separate ways. That was it. I never see her now, never write to her, don't even know where she is.

"She's the only woman I ever really loved."

Marge had the good sense to remain quiet. She was still picking at her salad, even though she hadn't eaten a mouthful during my talk. I hadn't either.

The food was cold. The waiter took it away. Finally over coffee Marge ventured:

"There might be others, Joe. All it takes is one."

I said nothing to that.

She lived close by, so I walked her back to her flat. It wasn't late, but I was dog tired. Maybe a bit shaken also.

She noticed that, and at the door of her building all she said was: "You better get some rest. You're all in."

I nodded. "Yeah. But I've had a very nice time."

"So have I," she smiled.

I bent down to give her a peck on the cheek, but at the last moment she turned my face so that our lips met. Only for a moment.

I gazed at her, a tangle of emotions running through me. She just looked back at me with a soft smile.

We said nothing for several moments. Then:

"I hope...I hope I can see you again sometime," I said hoarsely.

"I hope so too," she whispered.

Then she darted through the door without a backward glance.

I walked home, undressed, and slept like the dead.

CHAPTER NINETEEN

How to find the Removal Company? That was the last obstacle.

Sanderson had proved vulnerable: he had made a bad mistake in regard to the false memories he had implanted in Katharine Vance's mind. And if—as seemed likely—he had engineered the murder of Dr. Grabhorn, presumably to shut him up, he was not immune to panic. Strangely enough, I felt little worry for my own safety, even though Sanderson clearly had a large contingent of miscellaneous underlings to do his bidding.

But Sanderson himself continued to prove elusive. He had covered his tracks well. I couldn't come up with even the first step in tracing him—he was a phantom, a ghost, a man who blended in anonymously with the human tidal wave of a great city, who pulled strings from the center of his web like an immense, bloated spider.

Could he have ceased his operations? By this time he must surely have enough money to have retired many times over. As soon as I thought of the idea, I laughed it away: if Priscilla James of Pasadena had been one of his victims, he was still in business as of a few months ago.

He had changed his telephone number, but somehow I had a feeling that he was still in the same place he was when the Vances had seen him a year and a half ago. The Removal Company was an elaborate operation—that hexagonal white room at the top of a flight of stairs, a further room within, and God knows how many further compartments for the various other procedures Sanderson had to undertake after his victims had supposedly been put out of their misery.

Another mystery was why Sanderson didn't merely kill his victims rather than go through the incredible charade of imbuing them with a new personality. True, that would make him guilty of murder, and the disposal of corpses is not easy; but it nevertheless seemed easier than the Byzantine rigmarole he was engaging in. Did Sanderson get some bizarre kick out of being a puppet-master manipulating the lives of dozens, perhaps hundreds of people?

Although Vance had got his wife back, we needed to put Sanderson out of business: otherwise he would hover over his victims for the rest of their lives. There was no telling what he could, or would, do with the information he had at his disposal.

I had crawled into my office late in the morning, still exhausted from the cumulative rush of events over the last several weeks. The place looked dingy, so I rolled up the Venetian blinds, squinting at the bright April sunlight that met me full in the face.

I sat heavily at my desk. It was, as always, nearly bare. So was my mind. I was drawing a complete blank.

I fished the card for the Removal Company out of my suit pocket. In its mute blandness it seemed to mock me: a simple, euphemistic name and a disconnected phone number. Could I bribe someone at the phone company to check old records and see if there was an address attached to this number? Was that information even available?

I leaned back in my chair, the blazing sun striking me full in the back. I held the card up to the light.

Then I almost fell over in my haste to get up.

There was some other writing on the card—or, more properly, embossed on it. It was the bottom end of a double circle, and within the two curving lines was some writing.

A watermark.

All I could make out were the letters RBURY LAID. Not very helpful—but maybe enough for an expert. I wasn't one, but I knew someone who was.

I flew out of the office, took the stairs two at a time, and rushed out into the heat of an unusually warm New York spring day. In minutes I was at the door of my regular stationery store, Samuel Weiss at 154 West 32nd Street. They hadn't had much business from me lately, but I'd make sure to change that if they could be of help.

Sam himself was in the back of the shop, doing some typesetting work. Without ceremony I lifted the gate from the front counter and walked right back to him. He looked up at me first in momentary alarm, then with a wide grin of recognition.

"Joe! Where ya been all these mont's? Gone to one o' my competitors? I want your business, guy!"

"You'll get it," I said hurriedly. "Sam, you gotta—"

He held up a hand. "Just lemme finish this line, Joe," he said, bending back to his work. "I never was much good at setting woids backwards.... Man, you'd think they could come up with some better way—"

"Sam." The urgency in my voice brought back that look of alarm in Sam's face, and he quietly dropped some pieces of type and looked me straight in the face.

"What's the matter, Joe? You in some kinda trouble?"

"Not exactly. Just look at this." I handed him the card for the Removal Company.

He snickered at the name. "What is this, Joe? A garbage disposal outfit?"

"Jesus, Sam, will you cut the crap!" My harried tone wiped the grin off his face.

"I'm sorry, Joe." He peered at the card more intently. "What do you want to know? I'm pretty sure we didn't do this."

"I didn't think you did. But just hold the card up to the light, and tell me what you see."

He did as I asked, holding the lower left-hand corner of the card between thumb and forefinger and placing it under the bare light bulb directly above him.

"You see the watermark?" I said.

"Yeah, sure," he mumbled, now professionally interested.

"What is it? Can you tell?"

"Sure." He handed the card back to me nonchalantly. "Canterbury Laid. Pretty unusual."

"What does that mean?" I asked.

He shrugged. "Just a type of paper. Not often used in business cards—quite expensive, I'll have you know. See those tiny ridges across the card?"—rubbing the card gently back and forth as I held it in my hand—"That's what laid paper is. Most business cards of this kind are made with wove paper—helluva lot cheaper. So your pal here had a big wad o' dough to shell out for this baby."

"Do you know who could have made this?"

Weiss shrugged again. "I couldn't say for sure. But I'll tell you one thing: nine out of ten stationery stores or printers would have considered this out of their league. We don't even have any Canterbury Laid paper—too rich for our blood."

I thanked him hastily and left the place.

* * * * * * *

A quick check of the yellow pages revealed about six or seven establishments in the immediate vicinity where the card could have been made. I jotted them all down, then hit the road for another systematic canvass.

This time I was lucky. At the second place I visited—a small printer on First Avenue and 29th Street—I got the response I was hoping for. The printer's name was Bill Ford, and after looking at the card a few moments said:

"Yeah, this coulda been ours...."

When I pointed out the watermark, Ford became still more certain. "Yeah, yeah," he murmured, as if racking his brains. "It was years ago...five, six years ago at least...you know, we don't do business cards as a rule, but this guy was throwing a lot of money around, so we went ahead. He wanted the best paper he could get, and we had a big stock of Canterbury Laid stashed up for some limited-edition book...you know, one of those books 'for private distribution only'...." He chuckled.

"Do you remember what he looked like?" I said.

"No." Ford shook his head emphatically. "It's funny: I have a horrible memory for faces, but a pretty good one for *jobs*. This card rings a bell, but not the guy who ordered it."

"Could he possibly have had a new card made?" I asked. "This card is old—the phone number is inactive."

"I couldn't say," Ford replied. "Not to my knowledge."

I felt at a loss. I seemed so close.... But then Ford turned around and called out: "Harry! Hey, is Harry Wendelson there? Get over here!"

Presently a small, wiry fellow with thick glasses came up. "Yeah, boss?"

He took the card from me and showed it to Wendelson. "Look familiar to you?"

The underling looked at it for a moment, then beamed. "Yeah, sure, boss! The guy came in about a year ago—wanted a new card made, with a new phone number! Just like this, but a different number!"

I thought my heart was going to stop beating.

"Do you by chance have the invoice for that new order? Or even the old one?"

Ford said: "The old one—probably not. The new one, maybe so."

He led me into his office, at the back corner of the shop. Setting me down at his own desk, he grabbed a big file drawer bursting with slips of paper and dumped it in front of me.

"This is only arranged by date, not by name," Ford said. "But if Harry says it was about a year ago, then that might be the place to start."

It took me half an hour to find it. It was even more than I had hoped for. The name on the invoice read: *William Sampson, 548 Third Avenue*. A different name, but our man Sanderson clearly enjoyed a certain variety in his nomenclature.

But the thing I didn't expect was that the actual wording of the new business card was jotted down—whether in Sanderson's own hand or Ford's I didn't know, and it hardly mattered—right on the invoice.

It read:

THE REMOVAL COMPANY
MUrray Hill 6-9884

CHAPTER TWENTY

I wasn't by any means in the clear. I had no idea whether the address that Sanderson/Sampson had given was real or bogus. He would have no reason to give his real "business" address, since that wasn't going to be on the card.

All I could hope for was that Sanderson wouldn't think anyone would trouble to look up this invoice. Like most people, he probably lied only when it suited him; at other times it was simply less bother to tell the truth.

Anyway, it was all I had to go on. I had his current phone number, apparently, and that might be useful later, but right now I wanted to hunt the man himself down.

I did not overlook the irony that Sanderson's presumed place of business—548 Third Avenue, between 36th and 37th Streets—was about three blocks from my own office. But that wasn't important now. I had a lead—maybe—and needed to pursue it. For once using the luxury of a taxi, I had the guy take me right to the corner of Third and 36th.

It was not by any means a wealthy area, but it was clean and reputable. A good place for running a quietly nefarious practice. 548 was in the middle of the block, a nondescript four-story building juxtaposed between two buildings several stories higher. The first floor was a deli, if you can believe it.

That wasn't what interested me. That was just a front—or even, perhaps, a legitimate business. The stout, balding chap behind the cash register seemed entirely innocuous and perfectly at home in his surroundings. My interest was in what lay in the three stories above the store—and what, if anything, was behind it.

To that end I walked west along 36th Street, toward Lexington. About half way down the block I came to what I had hoped for—an alley separating the buildings facing Third Avenue from those on Lexington. Going down that narrow alley, scarcely large enough for a medium-sized car to traverse, I found myself looking at the back of the four-story building.

I looked long and hard. I made various calculations. A plan had begun to form.

* * * * * * *

A little past midnight saw me back in that alley, but this time with a certain quantity of supplies, chief of which was a stout rope at least thirty feet long.

My earlier examination had revealed that there were two separate doors at the back of 548, and both had deadbolt locks, so it would be hopeless to pick either of them. There were several windows, but the lowest one was still about twenty feet up. It also interested me that this was the only building on the block without a fire escape, even though the structures on either side of it were fully equipped with them.

The fire escape of the building to the right of 548 was a bit nearer to that lowest window than the one on the left. So I made my way there, leaping up to grab the last segment of the fire escape ladder and pulling it down. I climbed up to the third floor of the building and stopped to survey the territory.

It would be tough, and dangerous, but I didn't see what option I had.

I tied one end of the rope firmly to the metal railing of the fire escape and the other end around my own body. Then I climbed up on to the railing, paused there for a moment, and jumped.

My first attempt was a failure. I had gauged inaccurately, and only brushed the window-ledge of 548 with my hand before colliding painfully with the wall of the building and swinging back to the other building's fire escape. I was now hanging just below the fire escape on that building's second story. With difficulty I maneuvered myself up over the railing and went up one flight to try again.

The next go was better. I had seen that there was a metal projection—perhaps an attachment for a shutter—to the left of the window I was aiming for. I managed to grab it with my hand, even though its sharp edge caused a deep scratch on my left palm. For a moment I stood hanging there, legs flailing, right arm desperately scrabbling the brick wall feeling for some purchase. Finally my feet managed to reach the window-ledge and I hauled myself up. That shutter attachment was greasy with my own blood and difficult to hold on to, but I held fast while I gained my balance.

I waited a few moments for my heart to stop racing. I was breathing hard with exertion and adrenalin, and my whole body was quivering. It took minutes to get myself under control.

The window, as I had expected, was latched shut from the inside. I had come prepared for that. Reaching into a pouch I had attached to my waist, I took out a pencil to which I had attached a suction cup, and a glass cutter. My injured left hand was still gripping the metal attachment, so I had to place the pencil in my mouth while I worked the glass cutter.

After I had cut three edges of the pane nearest the window-latch, I placed the suction cup—still in my mouth—firmly on the glass, then cut the final edge. The pane popped out with unexpected vigor, and it snapped my head back so that I almost dropped it. But I held tight with my teeth. I put the glass cutter back in the pouch, carefully took the suction cup with the attached pane out of my mouth, and put that in the pouch also.

Then I reached through the window and unlatched it.

I still had only one hand with which to open the window. It had clearly not been opened for some time and proved recalcitrant. But with a grunt of effort I finally got it to budge. Levering it up from the bottom, I opened it as wide as it would go.

I rested my body half in and half out of the window, just as I had done in Dr. Grabhorn's house back in Pasadena. The room within was pitch dark, and I had no idea what was in it. My blind fumbling revealed nothing except cardboard boxes piled high on either side of the window. There seemed nothing directly below the window.

I had no choice but to crawl, as gently as I could, down the wall of that room from the window. I was hoping I could land gently on the floor, but that floor proved to be lower than I had bargained for, and after a time I slipped out of the window and fell with a heavy thud on the concrete floor.

I was stunned for several moments. My left arm had been pinned under me as I fell, and I had also hit my forehead hard on the floor. Even though I realized the need for quiet, I groaned aloud in pain and shock. For a fleeting instant I wanted to do nothing but lie there and go to sleep.

But I had to get up, and finally did so. I appeared to be in a store-room of some kind. Taking a flashlight out of my pouch, I cast it quickly around. The cardboard boxes seemed filled with medical supplies of various sorts—syringes, chemicals, test tubes, and the like. There was only a single door in the room, and I walked up to it.

I looked down at the floor and saw no light coming in through the crack of the door. So I took the knob in my uninjured hand and turned it—quietly and gently.

The room I now faced was completely empty save for a desk near its middle. It was shaped like a hexagon. Even in the darkness I could see that the entire room, including the desk, was painted white.

I was in the office of the Removal Company.

I didn't waste time examining the room I was in. It was, if Arthur Vance's description was sound, merely a kind of foyer. There would be another room—the one where he saw his wife Katharine, apparently dead, laid out on the hospital bed—and, beyond that, perhaps many other private rooms where Sanderson did his work.

The room I was in had several doors. One of them—to my right—must be the door at the top of the stairs leading up from the back door. Another, on the opposite end of the room and behind the desk, probably led to further offices.

I made for that door. I had no idea whether it might be locked or not, but somehow I doubted that it would be. It wasn't.

I was in that paneled room where Vance must have seen his "dead" wife. There were two doors leading off of this room also, and I paused irresolute over which one to try. The one on the left-hand wall was locked, so I abandoned it for the time being while I approached the door on the back wall.

It was unlocked.

I found myself facing an unexpectedly long hallway, with several doors on either side. My sense of perspective was thrown off: somehow it didn't seem as if this building was big enough to accommodate so many rooms. Each of them must have been quite small.

It was only now that I pulled out my gun.

Most of the doors had small windows roughly at eye level; but their interiors were uniformly dark, and I could see nothing in them. Every door I tried was locked.

Finally, at the end of the hall, I saw a door without any window in it. I cautiously tried the knob. It moved. The door was unlocked.

It was only moments after I had entered that room that I felt the heavy impact on my neck that sent me into oblivion.

CHAPTER TWENTY-ONE

The throbbing in my head and neck was almost unendurable. I thought I might be violently ill if I tried to get up, so I did nothing but lie back on the mattress and rest my head on the soft pillow. There was an antiseptic smell in the air, but it was not unpleasant. I felt weak as a dishrag; my heart seemed to be racing, and tremors were running up and down my entire body, especially my arms and legs. Minutes after I opened my eyes in the dimness, I tried gingerly to get up.

I found that I was bound to a hospital bed with firm leather straps that pinned down my arms, legs, and body. It was all I could do to move my head forward a few inches.

I lay back again, exhausted and frustrated. I had been a perfect fool. Utterly careless. The seeming desertion of the place had caused me to let down my guard.

I had no idea what lay in store for me, but I was prepared for the worst. Vance had called Sanderson a "fiend" and a "devil," and it now appeared that he was right.

The door of the small, narrow room I was in opened. A shadowy figure entered. It was Dr. Sanderson.

He did not turn on the light, for which I was relieved—it probably would have blinded me. But in the darkness—pierced only by a faint glow coming from somewhere far away down the corridor—Sanderson looked blurred, hazy, as if the outlines of his body were not well defined.

"Ah," he said, "Mr. Scintilla, I see you have awoken. I trust you'll pardon the injury I inflicted upon you. I am not accustomed to invaders."

"Don't mention it." I really didn't feel like bandying words with the fellow, but apparently I had no choice.

He pulled up a wooden chair and sat down in it. In that position his head was actually a bit lower than my supine body, and he had to look up at me. The dim glow from the corridor lit up his face eerily.

"You have been most industrious, Mr. Scintilla. It does appear as if you have probed nearly all my secrets."

"Have I?" I said weakly. "There are plenty of things I still don't know."

"You'd like some explanations?" Sanderson said, smirking slightly.

I gave as good an imitation of a shrug as I could manage. "The biggest question, doctor, is why. What's your game? What are you really trying to do?"

Sanderson got up abruptly and began walking about the room. "My dear sir, that could be taken in a number of ways. Exactly what do you mean? You wish to discuss my philosophy, or my methods?"

"Maybe a bit of both."

He almost grinned. "Yes, I now recall...you are a student of philosophy, are you not? Johns Hopkins, I believe?"

I said nothing. He had clearly done his homework.

"Perhaps, Mr. Scintilla, it might be best if *you* told *me* what it is that I am trying to do. I will then supplement or amend your account as needed."

I felt strangely as if I were back in college, with a professor tutoring me in his office.

"All right," I said. "Some of it I get, some of it I don't.... You know, it might be helpful if you untied me. This is mighty uncomfortable."

Sanderson looked at me with a sort of mild benevolence. "You are so right, Mr. Scintilla. Please forgive me."

And he undid all the leather straps around me. In doing so he made it pretty clear that he had a revolver in a holster around his chest. But he knew I wasn't planning anything: I was so weak that I could do little but stretch my body around a bit.

Then I noticed that a bandage had been placed on my left hand.

Sanderson saw my glance. "You were bleeding rather badly there, I'm sorry to say."

Without looking at him I said: "Thanks."

There was silence for several moments. Then:

"All right, Dr. Sanderson, if that's your name"—he merely smiled at that—"here's what I figure is going on. You have a lot of people—psycho-analysts, servants, maybe even regular doctors—who funnel potentially suicidal people to you. You claim to help them put an end to their lives easily and painlessly, at the same time exacting immense fees from them for the service. But instead of killing them, you first give them some kind of drug that gives them the appearance of death; then, when you revive them, you perform some kind of hypnotism so that they take on someone else's personality. Right so far?"

He said: "I will admit that there is a great deal more to it than that, but in essence that is correct."

"All right. But what I don't get is: how do you plant the 'new' personalities? When you turned Katharine Vance into Elena Cavalieri, how did you get her into the Greenway household, and how did you get Harry Greenway to marry her?"

Sanderson actually laughed. "My good man, that is the easiest part of the procedure. Do you know anything about Mr. Harry Greenway—or rather, his father?" I shook my head. "He was a very rich man—and he became rich in ways that are...shall we say, somewhat unsavory? It was child's play to collect certain—information—on him so that he was persuaded to take in his long-lost second cousin and eventually marry her. Perhaps he even loved her: she is, as you know, very beautiful."

"So," I said, "in addition to all your other activities, you're a blackmailer."

Sanderson gave me a mildly exasperated look, as if I were a doltish schoolboy. "Mr. Scintilla, you weary me. I do not think you quite grasp what it is that I am trying to do. You yourself—I know from my research—have no love lost for the wealthy among us; neither do I. There is scarcely a wealthy man in America, or the world, who does not have something he wishes to hide; and if I can make use of that something for the benefit of others, then I shall do so."

He suddenly brought his face close to mine.

"Do you take me for an evil man? Do you think that what I do is criminal, morally reprehensible, nefarious? Let me tell you how *I* look at things, and perhaps you will think differently."

He began pacing again.

"There are, Mr. Scintilla, a great many people in this world who are unhappy. Perhaps they have an incurable illness; perhaps they are suffering from unassuaged grief; or perhaps they are simply morose, depressed, cheerless—facing long years of misery, tedium, and uselessness.

"You are a philosopher, Mr. Scintilla. Do you not remember your Schopenhauer? 'The conviction that the world and man is something that had better not have been, is of a kind to fill us with indulgence towards one another.... Human life must be some kind of mistake.' Think deeply about that utterance, Mr. Scintilla: *Human life must be some kind of mistake.* Now I do not go quite that far. I myself derive considerable pleasure out of existence—but there are those who do not. And you know as well as I that I have never—*never*—'assisted' someone who did not genuinely wish to die.

"Mr. Scintilla, people are weak. They are irresolute, indecisive, incapable of taking control of their own lives. To engineer one's death is the best, the noblest thing a human being can do. It is the ultimate expression of self-sufficiency. Suicide is never cowardly, it is always brave. The Romans knew that; the Japanese samurai knew that. All I do is to assist such people—or, rather, give them that illusion."

"But you *don't* kill them, do you? Have you ever 'assisted' anyone in committing suicide?"

"Not a one," he said proudly. "What I had told Mr. Vance on this subject was quite true: I would be foolish to do such a thing, for it would have brought me to the gallows long ago. Do you think I would risk my own life in that way even for immense sums of money? I would be mad to do so."

"Then why do you extort such a fee? You must have made millions by now."

"Extort? Come now. In the first place, the large sums I *request* my wealthier clients to pay are well within their resources, and moreover they are required to foster the deception that their loved ones really are being...removed. So too that rigmarole about signing the paper implicating the surviving party—in your case, Mr. Arthur Vance—as an 'accessory' in my 'crime.'

"In the second place, my man, that fee is quite variable. Do you truly imagine that I only seek wealthy clients? That would be barbaric. I am not a money-grubber. I turn no one away, and in some cases my fee is very modest. Why"—with a twisted smile—"I suspect even you could afford it. I am always happy to make special allowances."

This was rapidly getting tiresome. Sanderson was beginning to sound like some kind of mad scientist. And yet, there was something not quite right here: he seemed to be putting on an act, with his precise, stilted manner of speaking. It wasn't him; it sounded phony. He was trying to hide something.

"But why give your 'victims' the personalities of someone else?" I said. "It seems awfully cumbersome."

"It is *very* cumbersome, Mr. Scintilla. But creating a person out of whole cloth would be far more so. In this Vance matter, the death of the real Elena Cavalieri and her parents seemed to present a golden opportunity. I hope you don't think I had anything to do with that regrettable accident?"

I said nothing. The thought had indeed crossed my mind.

"It was not likely," Sanderson continued, "that anyone knew anything about the Cavalieris, and they really were cousins of the Greenways, as you have discovered, so no one would think anything of it when Harry Greenway took poor Elena under his wing. Were it not for that boating accident, Mrs. Vance may have gone somewhere else altogether: I had a number of other possibilities in my files....

"Once again, you do not quite grasp the entire picture—nor, indeed, the difficulties involved. You refer to my 'hypnotism.' That is far too crude a term for what I actually do. It takes months, Mr. Scintilla, *months* to indoctrinate my 'victim,' as you term it, into his or her new personality. That labor alone justifies my high fees. The old personality must be wiped out entirely—or, at any rate, covered over completely with the new one. Memories, reaching back to childhood, modes of behavior, down to the smallest instinctive gestures—all these things take an immense amount of time and effort."

"But you slipped up there, Sanderson. You didn't quite do the job. Katharine Vance *thought* she had Elena Cavalieri's memories of growing up in Italy, but she didn't recognize the very house she had lived in."

Sanderson exhaled heavily. "Sir, there are limits even to my thoroughness. I managed to make her a false passport and visa, and to have that false immigration record planted at Ellis Island—that was child's play, given the low salaries those poor officials receive—but I had no expectation that someone like you would trouble to go all the way to Italy to check Miss Cavalieri's background. Your industry is to be praised, Mr. Scintilla, however awkward it may be to me."

Now I felt like a schoolboy who, much to the teacher's surprise, had come up with a right answer.

"The fact is," he continued, "that it was not entirely your own doggedness and ingenuity that caught me in my deception, but an unfortunate series of accidents. If Mr. Vance had not seen that clipping from the newspaper—yes, I know all about that—he would never have come to you, and we would not be here right now. In truth, most of 'clients'—or, rather, their survivors—do not trouble to pursue such matters. They have long since resigned themselves to the departure of their loved ones, and when those loved ones are in fact out of the way, that is usually the end of it. Most people would wish to forget such things as quickly as possible."

I had to shut Sanderson up—shake him up, jolt him.

"How about Grabhorn?" I said. "Did he have to die?"

That did the trick. Sanderson wheeled about—almost seemed in a panic.

"You were getting too close, Scintilla! That was *your* doing! It was *you* who condemned him to death!"

His outburst surprised me. "You couldn't think of any other way of keeping him quiet?"

Sanderson snapped: "He was trying to flee! He had already changed his name—as if that would have thrown me off the scent for more than a moment—but he had too much information.... He was terrified, wanted to back out of our—our relationship. I couldn't let him do that. He was fundamentally an unstable man, and might have brought me down with him.

"So when that receptionist whom I had placed to keep an eye on him reported your visit to me, I felt he had to go."

I now remembered something Grabhorn had said: *"Why can't you people leave me alone?"* The remark made no sense if applied to Vance and me—we hadn't bothered him before. He must have been repeatedly hounded by Sanderson's underlings. I turned back to him.

"I don't imagine you pulled the trigger yourself."

Sanderson looked actually horrified. "Good God, no! Surely you know there are many people who...who can be persuaded to do that."

Sanderson began pacing the little room again. He seemed very uncomfortable with this subject.

"So what happens now?" I said. "Am I your next victim?"

He glared at me with narrowed eyes. "I repeat to you, Mr. Joseph Scintilla, that I have never killed anyone in all my career. And I do not intend to start now."

"So what's the game? You're not just going to let me go free."

Sanderson smiled slowly. "Why, yes, my dear man, I am going to do exactly that."

I peered at him in the darkness, trying to figure out his meaning.

"But first," he resumed, in an efficient, businesslike way, "I hope you will not mind if I put these straps back on for just a moment. They will be fastened firmly, but not uncomfortably."

He did as he said, then left the room.

In a few moments he returned, with a syringe in his hand. Hardly looking at me, he tested it briefly, found it satisfactory, then said: "Please don't struggle, Mr. Scintilla, it will only do you harm."

He inserted the needle into my arm.

Within minutes, I felt extremely strange.... I was floating...my head seemed detached from my body...vision blurred...thought I was going to be sick...couldn't focus...Sanderson...was that him...? What... someone talking....

"You will find Mr. Arthur Vance and his wife and kill them without delay. You will find Mr. Arthur Vance and his wife and kill them without delay. You will find Mr. Arthur Vance...."

Over and over...like a dream...nightmare...inside my head...beating, pounding, throbbing...inside my head...head bursting...kill...Vance...wife... kill....

CHAPTER TWENTY-TWO

I crawled into my office late in the morning. I felt terrible. The residual effects of that exhausting trip to Italy must still be affecting me. I had a pain in the back of my neck that I couldn't account for; must have slept funny last night.

The case seemed to have come to a standstill. Sure, Vance had his wife back, but we were no closer to getting Sanderson than before—and we needed to get him. This evil puppet-master would be lurking in the shadows for the rest of their lives if he wasn't stopped. And if the case of Priscilla James of Pasadena was what we thought it was, then the Removal Company was still very much in business.

But how to find the fellow? He had covered his tracks too well. All we had was that bland business card with the disconnected phone number in Murray Hill.

I fished around in the pockets of my wrinkled suit. Now I couldn't even find the goddamn card. I scanned my nearly empty desk, opening drawers uselessly. Must have fallen out—or maybe Vance had it. Well, it couldn't possibly be of any use anyway.

I felt a need to talk to Arthur Vance. I didn't know what more he could possibly tell me, but it seemed imperative for me to see him. Maybe his wife could remember something of what she had gone through, although probably she was still so traumatized that it would be unwise to question her.

I got Vance on the phone.

"Scintilla here," I said. "How are you feeling?"

"All right," he said, a little nervously. Maybe he didn't expect even this much solicitude from me—it's not my custom. "Haven't been sleeping very well."

"Nor I. How about Mrs. Vance?"

"The doctor has her pretty well sedated most of the time. She's up for short periods during the day."

"You think she's going to make it?"

"God, I hope so, Joe!" Vance burst out. "I think her memories—you know, memories of *herself,* not of this Elena woman—are coming back, slowly...very slowly. I really need to take her back to California, but the doctor says she couldn't stand such a long trip right now. And anyway, I guess we still have to finish this thing...."

"That's what I want to talk to you about. You gonna be home? I'm coming over."

"But—but what more can I do?" Vance stammered.

"I'm not sure. We just got to put our heads together. Just sit tight; I'm on my way."

I rang off. Before leaving the office I tried to brush out the dust and wrinkles from my suit, but didn't have much luck. God, it seemed as if I'd slept in it.

At the door of my office I stopped abruptly, turned back, opened the lowest right-hand drawer of my desk, and slipped my .22 in my pocket. Don't know why I did that; I just felt better with it.

* * * * * * *

Vance was there, looking frazzled and worried. Dr. Williamson was also there, just coming out of the room where Katharine was resting. Before he closed the door I saw a nurse sitting at her bedside.

Marge Schaeffer was there too, sitting quietly on the couch.

Vance offered me coffee, which I accepted. Maybe it would help to shake the cobwebs from my head. I still felt as if I'd slept for a year—brain wasn't working right. Couldn't think clearly.

I sat down next to Marge and gave her a little squeeze. But I quickly turned my attention back to Arthur Vance.

"Listen, we have to find Sanderson. But we haven't the faintest idea how to track him down. I was wondering whether your wife might be able to tell us something—"

Dr. Williamson, who by this time had put on his coat and hat and was almost out the door, stopped abruptly.

"Now hold on a minute, Mr. Scintilla. That would be very unwise. Mrs. Vance is in a very disturbed state—trauma and partial amnesia, just for starters—and she cannot answer any questions. I forbid it, sir!"

He stood there with his chest expanded, as if he himself would physically stop me.

"Okay, doc," I said placatingly, "it was just a thought."

"In any case," he said, relenting a bit, "she is sedated. She won't be talking to anyone for hours."

"Any chance when she *might* be ready to talk?"

Williamson looked exasperated. "Mr. Scintilla, I will acknowledge that I do not know what this is about. I have not been informed"—he glared briefly at Vance—"how Mrs. Vance has suddenly emerged, after having 'disappeared' a year and a half ago, nor what she has been through. But she is now my patient, and I have to do the best I can for her. It may be weeks—months—before she can tell of her experiences, whatever they may be."

With that, he grabbed the doorknob and made as if to leave, but stopped short and turned back to Vance.

"Arthur, I will hold you responsible if anything is done to disturb your wife. If you have any concern for her, you will not let that happen."

"I won't, doctor. I promise."

"Very well."

Williamson stormed out huffily.

"Well," I said, "so much for that." I walked about the room impatiently. "But listen, we have to find Sanderson! Arthur, can't you say *anything* more about where you were taken in that Packard that day?"

"Joe, don't you remember? I was blindfolded! Both times! I hadn't a clue where we went. And anyway, who's to say that Sanderson is even in that same place any more? That old phone number is disconnected, so maybe he's somewhere else altogether!"

"That's true," I murmured. "By the way: where's that card for the Removal Company? Do you have it?"

"No, of course not," Vance said, brow furrowing. "I gave it to you."

"Well, it doesn't matter. It's not important."

We all stood about irresolutely. The coffee hadn't helped my brain any. Everything still seemed a mush.

My hand wanted to reach into my pocket. It was as if I had no control over it. Something strange was happening. I dug my hand into my pocket and pulled out the gun.

For a moment I looked at it in bewilderment—it could have been somebody else's gun, or somebody else's hand.

I pointed it at Arthur Vance.

All he did was laugh. "What's the joke, Scintilla? You been watching too many cops and robbers movies?"

I was muttering something—I could hardly make out the words myself. "...kill...Vance...wife...."

Marge burst out: "Joe, put that thing away. You might hurt someone."

She came forward as if to disarm me. I wheeled around and pointed the gun right at her midsection.

"Get away from me!" I shouted. "Leave me alone! Leave me alone...." That last sentence sounded more like a whine than a command.

Marge stopped abruptly, concern and alarm all over her face. "Joe, what's going on? Are you not well? Please...."

I put my hands over my ears. "Stop it! Just leave me alone! I don't want to hurt you, Marge...it's not you I'm after."

I hardly knew what I was saying. The words didn't seem to be coming from my mouth.

Marge and Arthur flashed looks of consternation at each other, but didn't move or say anything.

I hurled myself toward the double doors where Katharine Vance was resting. Thrusting them open, I pointed my gun at the nurse within and barked at her:

"Get out, lady! Scram! Beat it! Right this minute!"

With a little scream she flew up out of her chair and dashed into the living room. She halted there uncertainly until I screamed:

"Get out! Now!"

She opened the door and left the place without a backward glance.

"You too, Marge," I said, waving the gun at her.

She didn't budge. "Joe, please...what's come over you? You're not well—something's terribly wrong. Please don't do this...."

I stalked up to her. I was ready to blow her away also. I had never felt so enraged in all my life.

Marge actually reached out and stroked my cheek. "Joe," she whispered, "please stop. Please...."

I thrust her away from me and almost dragged her to the door. "Get out, I said! Right now!"

With one look at Vance and another at me, she left the place, leaving the door open.

I turned back to the only other occupant of the room. "Okay, Vance, this is it. Into the bedroom."

Still looking at me in complete bewilderment, he marched like a zombie into the room. It was pretty dark—only a small night-light on. Katharine Vance was sleeping on the bed peacefully.

"It's the finish, Vance. I gotta do this."

I pointed my gun at his chest.

"Joe, why?" he said softly. "What have I done...?"

"Just shut up."

But my hand started to quiver, then my arm, then my whole body. I was like a man with ague, or St. Vitus's dance. The dim outlines of the room began to swim in front of my eyes. Why the hell couldn't I pull the trigger? I had to pull it—my brain was giving me the command to pull it—but I couldn't.

I shifted about and aimed the gun at Katharine. My hand was still shaking so much that I tried to steady it with the other hand, but it was no good. My heart seemed to be beating irregularly. I could feel beads of sweat all over me.

Vance saw the direction of my gun and almost shrieked, "No, Joe!" and flung himself in front of his wife. She continued to sleep in complete tranquility. "Shoot me if you have to, man, but not her! Not her!"

"You're both gonna get it," I said in an undertone. "I gotta do this...gotta do this...."

Vance suddenly stood up straight, stone-faced. "Do it, then. Do it, Joe. Go ahead."

My hand was now shaking so much that I almost dropped the gun. I had to get through with this—after that I would have peace. I knew that the throbbing in my brain would end as soon as I pulled the trigger twice. That's all I had to do.

My index finger finally seemed about to respond. It was drawing back the trigger. Drawing it back....

Then I aimed the gun at my own head and fired.

CHAPTER TWENTY-THREE

My head hurt.

When I opened my eyes and saw myself on a hospital bed, I momentarily panicked—thought I was back in the office of the Removal Company. But I quickly saw that this was a real hospital—probably the recently opened New York Hospital on Marie Curie Avenue—and sank back on the bed in relief. Then I noticed that there were other people in the room.

Arthur Vance, Gene Merriwether, and—sitting demurely in a chair reading a magazine—Marge Schaeffer.

Vance saw that my eyes were open and quickly summoned a nurse. She came in running and checked me over. "How are you feeling, Mr. Scintilla?" she said.

"Okay," I grunted. I held my hand up to my head—it was bandaged all around. "What exactly has happened to me?"

"I think you'd better let your friends explain that," she said as she made to leave the room. "But remember—not too much excitement." Her glance took us all in.

It looked as if no one knew where to start, so I took the initiative. Things were starting to come back—the cobwebs were being cleared from my head.

"I remember...I remember finding Sanderson's office...he caught me...drugged me...tried to make me do something...." I looked up at Vance.

"Yes," he said, "we figured it was something like that. You nearly blew my head off—and my wife's too, for that matter." He grinned as if it were a big joke.

"Sanderson had given me some kind of hypnotic command," I resumed. "I guess he figured that would be the simplest way to dispose of us all. But I know a little bit about hypnosis—had talked about it with some medical student at Johns Hopkins years ago. It's next to impossible to get someone under hypnosis to do something they don't naturally want to do. So when Sanderson gave me that command, it just didn't work—set up this conflict in me, I guess. And so...."

"And so," Vance picked up, "you pulled the trigger on yourself to short-circuit the mental conflict you were in."

"Yes, that must be it," I said. "But...uh, pardon my asking, but if that's so, why am I not dead? Was my aim that bad?"

"Oh, no," said Vance, "it was pretty good—or would have been if not for this lady."

He gestured to Marge, who was still sitting in the chair, but now looking right at me.

"You...," I stammered. "Marge...how...?"

"You didn't think I was just going to leave you in that situation, did you?" she said tartly, with a bit of a reproach. "You ordered me to leave, but I didn't. I just hung outside the door. When you went into the bedroom with Arthur, I crept back in. And then, when you turned that gun on yourself, I rushed up from behind and managed to pull your arm up at the last minute. But I think you still grazed yourself. You have a nice groove up the side of your hard head, I think."

I reached up and gently felt the right-hand side of my head through the bandages. She was right.

"Um...thanks, I guess," I said without looking at her.

"You *guess?*" She was still ribbing me. "You don't really mean you wanted to blow your brains out? That's all the gratitude I get for saving your life?"

"I didn't mean it like that," I said hastily. "You *did* save my life, and I'm thankful."

"Well," she said with a smile, "I guess I was being a little selfish too. I want you to stick around a little longer."

With that, she suddenly bent over and gave me a quick kiss on the lips.

I must have turned beet red; my face got all hot.

Vance was smirking. "All right, lovebirds," he said, "I'll leave you two alone. Come on, Gene, let's scram." He took his friend and marched off.

At the door of the room he stopped. "But we'll be back when you're...er, better. We have things to do, don't we?"

"Yes," I said, grimly. "We do."

* * * * * *

We were sitting in the apartment of Arthur Vance's uncle. A few more days had gotten me on my feet—sufficiently, at any rate, to stumble out of the hospital in spite of the doctor's protests. I still had a bandage—a smaller one—wrapping the side of my head, but with my hat on it was pretty inconspicuous.

Vance was there, of course, along with Marge and Gene. I wasn't sure how exactly these two had insinuated themselves into the affair, but it seemed that Vance had told them pretty much everything. They may have been there merely to lend moral support; or perhaps they pictured themselves lending support of a more active kind, although I couldn't quite see how that was possible.

Putting Sanderson out of commission was the only goal that remained. Now that his hypnotic command had worn off, everything about my experience in the office of the Removal Company had come flooding back. I also found the scrap of paper on which I had written his current phone number, from that printer's invoice.

But the problem remained: How to get him?

Could we just burst into the place and expect to gun him down? Who knew what kind of security or protection he had? In my midnight escapade I hadn't seen the fellow Vance had called Bullet Head, but it was likely enough that he or some similar stooge was there—maybe others, as well. Sanderson may or may not have figured out that his attempt to use me to dispose of the Vances hadn't worked: he would surely have noticed that no account of their deaths had appeared in the papers. So he might be doubly on guard for some further attack.

We needed to counteract his guile with superior guile of our own. But how?

Our brainstorming session wasn't turning up much. Neither Vance nor I could approach Sanderson directly—he knew us too well by now. And there would be no more secret-agent climbing in through second-story windows. The whole problem was infuriatingly tantalizing: we knew where Sanderson was, but couldn't do anything about it.

That was when Marge Schaeffer said:

"Well, there's one possibility...."

"What?" at least two of us said, desperate to hear any new suggestion.

"We could send in some guinea pigs into the Removal Company...."

"To do what?" I said. "He has at least one bodyguard, possibly more. How are one or two people going to contend with them?"

"There's a way, I think, if you'd hear me out."

"There may be," I countered, "but it's too risky. And anyway, who could we possibly entrust with a mission like that?"

"How about us?" Marge said, in a small voice, gesturing to Gene and herself.

"Absolutely not!" I exploded. "Are you crazy? I am not going to have you—either of you"—I flashed a look at Gene—"march into that office and not be able to come out. No!"

"But, Joe, it may be the only way to get him...."

"Then we *won't* get him! I am not going to put you in harm's way. Sanderson may have said he hadn't killed anybody before, but we have no way of knowing whether he's telling the truth or not. He's a madman—and a brilliant madman at that, which makes it worse. I *will not* have you in his clutches!" I was breathing irregularly, glaring at her.

She looked down at her feet. "It's sweet of you, Joe, to be so concerned, but there may not be any other way." She held up her hand to still my impending protest. "And anyway, it won't be just Gene and me. If you'll listen to the plan, maybe you'll think differently about it."

I listened. I really didn't think much differently about it, but the others seemed willing to put it into action. I was outvoted.

But as I listened, I began to get very nervous. This was going to be a long shot, and could end in disaster for us all.

* * * * * * *

"All right," said Gene, hanging up the phone. "It's him. His man will be here in twenty minutes."

So far, so good. Sanderson had taken the bait—I hoped. Given his apparently extensive cadre of spies, underlings, and collaborators, I had begun to be uneasy that he might know of Marge and Gene and their relation to Vance and myself; but that was a chance we had to take.

I had chosen the Plaza Hotel, near the southeast corner of Central Park, as the rendezvous for the next "clients" of the Removal Company: its large, semi-circular driveway would make it easier to pursue the car that Sanderson would send to fetch Marge and Gene. Vance had suggested that he and I merely wait near the Removal Company's office on Third Avenue, but I had rejected that idea: in the unlikely event that our friends were taken somewhere else, we would have no way of tracking them. I was a professional in shadowing people, either on foot or in a car; and thought I could escape detection in hunting our quarry down.

Vance and I were already in our vehicle—a Renault Primastella belonging to Arthur's uncle—when we saw Marge and Gene come out of the hotel and wait on the sidewalk. In minutes a black Packard ambled in and quietly pulled up to them. A man got out of the car.

Vance grabbed my arm excitedly. "That's—"

"Yes, I know. That's Bullet Head."

Incongruously, he shook hands with both Marge and Gene before ushering them into the back seat of his car. With an inconspicuous gesture he pulled out two black silk handkerchiefs and gave some instructions his charges. He was standing directly in front of the door of the back seat, so it was next to impossible for anyone to see or make sense of his actions. No one—and there were plenty of other people in the vicinity in this sunny late afternoon in April—noticed what he did. But we were prepared for it, and we saw it all.

Bullet Head got into the driver's seat and pulled out slowly. We followed.

As expected, he took an extraordinarily circuitous route to his destination, at one time going as far east as Sutton Place and another time as far west as Times Square. Without exception his driving was moderate, calm, and entirely collected. He gave no indication that he knew he was being followed.

The Packard finally pulled up at the alley off 36th Street. With impeccable control, Bullet Head pulled the car up virtually to the back door of 548 Third Avenue. It would have been folly to have followed him in, so we parked on the street a little farther down and quickly got out of our vehicle. Vance nearly blundered right into the alley, but I grabbed him at the last minute:

"Stay back, you fool! They haven't gone in yet!"

By craning my head infinitesimally around the edge of the building at the mouth of the alley, I could see all I needed to see. The alley was so narrow that Bullet Head had had some difficulty getting out of his side of the car. Finally managing it, he walked stiffly around the back of the car, gave a quick look around, then opened the back seat door. Marge and Gene got out clumsily. Bullet Head gestured for them to stand still while he opened the door leading up to the Removal Company with a succession of keys.

All three went in.

After about a minute Vance and I crept into the alley and placed ourselves around the door our friends had entered. If anyone had been in that storeroom directly above, through whose window I had climbed several days ago, they would have spotted us instantly. I looked up, seeing the empty space where the pane I had removed had been. The window was dark.

This was now the hard part. We would have to wait. The plan was for Gene to let Marge actually go with Sanderson into the inner office of the Removal Company, then—with the gun he had taken with him—overpower Bullet Head and let us in. I had no idea how long this whole process would take: Sanderson would have to go through his customary procedure of "counseling" Marge to make sure that her "decision" was irrevocable, there would be the signing of papers, and all that business. It was difficult to estimate how long we should wait: fifteen minutes? twenty? half an hour? And what if Gene should fail in his mission? What if Bullet Head overwhelmed him?

I did not want to contemplate that possibility, both for his sake and for Marge's.

But we had to have some alternative plan. Frankly, there would be nothing to it except to blast our way in. Vance had brought his cannon of a gun, and that might do. But we had two heavy, deadbolted doors to go through, and such an entrance couldn't be made quietly. Who knows what appalling fate would await Marge and Gene—and ourselves—if Sanderson heard such a commotion and realized the plot against him?

So we waited.

Vance, inevitably, was impatient. After five minutes he already wanted to do something—anything—but I hissed in his face to keep his mouth shut. I had to confess I wasn't feeling very patient or confident myself. Gene was a newspaper man; could he be a match for a toughened bodyguard, even one who might be caught off-guard? It was the one weak link in the plan, but there had been no way around it.

After ten minutes my palms were moist with sweat, and my finger was slipping greasily over the trigger of my gun. Vance was almost exploding with frustration, whispering impotently:

"For God's sake, Joe, we gotta do something! It may be too late already...."

"No," I said, putting forth an assurance I hardly felt. "Give it more time. You remember how long it took for Katharine to go—"

"It didn't take this long!" Vance said almost out loud. "Marge... Gene...they could be—"

"Shut the bloody hell up, will you?" I spit out. "Just shut up and wait."

We waited.

Suddenly a sense of the utter unreality of what we were doing came over me. A great city's incessant hum of traffic sounded all around us. A few people actually crossed the mouth of the alley, entirely oblivious of what was going on only a few hundred feet away. Children were coming home from school, laughing and roughhousing. A stray cat came into the alley, sniffing for food.

I couldn't take it any more. "All right," I said. "We're going in."

We were about to turn our guns on the door when it suddenly

opened.

Bullet Head faced us, staring at us entirely without expression.

"What the—" Vance burst out.

He was about to turn his gun on the man when, like a ghost or shadow, Gene Merriwether loomed up behind him. Bullet Head grunted, feeling something digging into his back.

"Come on up, you guys!" Gene said quickly. "You gotta move fast—he's got Marge!"

We flew up the stairs.

I was the first one in the door leading into that white, hexagonal room, but Vance was right behind me. When he entered, he suddenly seemed to choke, then started to quiver all over. He must have been remembering.

I didn't have time for that. Seeing Gene and Bullet Head lumber up behind us, I turned to Vance and whispered: "Cover him! Tie him up if you can."

I made my way to the door leading into that paneled room. As I was about to turn the knob, I paused irresolutely. I tried to hear what was going on inside, but no sounds emerged.

Then I flung the door open.

Sanderson had just finished injecting something into Marge; the syringe was still in his hand. She was lying on a hospital bed, supine and utterly motionless. Sanderson looked up in sudden alarm at my entrance. The air of sardonic tranquility he always tried to maintain vanished instantly.

"You—you filthy scum!" he shouted.

Flinging the syringe away, he fled through a door and into that long corridor I remembered from my last visit.

Vance now burst in. At sight of Marge he covered his mouth with his hand. "Oh, my God—"

"It's all right, Vance! He's just drugged her. She'll come around. I'm going after him!"

Without waiting for a response, I rushed into the corridor.

I had my quarry in sight, and this time I wasn't going to lose him.

CHAPTER TWENTY-FOUR

The long corridor was only dimly lit with weak, flickering bulbs that caused both Sanderson's shadow and my own to drape the narrow walls eerily as we flew past. The many doors on either side of the hall were closed, but their little windows offered some further feeble illumination, possibly from windows within. I could have sworn that a couple of them were occupied, with male and female bodies laid out like corpses in a morgue. I tried my damnedest not even to guess who they might be.

Sanderson turned abruptly to the left at the very last door; it slammed to, and then there was another hard click whose implication I didn't grasp until I reached it myself seconds later. It was a deadbolt. Peering through the small window in the door, I saw that it was a set of stairs leading both up and down. Sanderson was already out of sight.

"Damn!" I spit out.

There was no recourse. I pointed my gun directly at the deadbolt and fired. The explosion was immense, far greater than I had expected—it reverberated off the walls of the corridor, sending me reeling backward to crash into the door behind me. I grunted in pain, but nevertheless saw that my shot had done the trick. The door had flipped open.

I had enough remnants of caution not to rush through it; instead, a peered carefully both up and down those concrete stairs, looking either for a trace of Sanderson, if he had continued to flee, or for a gun leveled at me, on the chance that he had decided to make this his stakeout for a final confrontation.

I saw nothing, but thought I could just detect the sound of footsteps—coming from below, and receding increasingly into the distance.

I flew down the stairs. At the second bend I just caught a glimpse of him going through a door. Possibly I could have taken a potshot at him, but I had a certain scruple about shooting a man—any man, even a criminal or fugitive—in the back. My chances of hitting him were in any case not good.

I thought I had reached that door at the foot of the stairs only seconds after he had, but when I opened it—again cautiously—I saw that it led to the alley, and that Sanderson had already entered his black Packard and was setting it in motion. Just as I reached the alley myself, the car took off screechingly, its sides showering sparks as they brushed grindingly against the brick and concrete buildings on either side of the narrow passage.

I fired a couple of shots, aiming for his tires, but apparently missed. Sanderson had gone forward, exiting the alley at 37th Street and turning hard to the right; his car nearly fishtailed as he did so. Cursing again, I ran back the other way toward Vance's uncle's car, leaped in, and took off after him.

I didn't attempt to navigate that alley, but instead pulled up to the corner of 36th and Lexington Avenue. Sanderson's car was easy to spot, and I saw it heading north on Lexington. I followed.

Things now started to get bizarre.

Sanderson did not floor his gas pedal as I had expected, but proceeded with a certain quiet urgency, weaving around slower-moving vehicles but not doing anything that could be considered reckless. I quickly concluded that he was anxious not to attract the attention of the police, and in the next moment realized that it would be to my advantage not to do so as well. If the law were brought in now, the explanations involved would be fearsomely complicated, and might possibly be irreparably damaging to my client and perhaps to hundreds of others—all those people who had used the "services" of the Removal Company. There was every reason to try to resolve this business quietly and privately.

And so I too proceeded with caution, making sure to keep Sanderson in my sights but not making any sudden or dangerous move that would bring on a siren. A busy street was not the place to bring this matter to a head.

Sanderson was heading north, eternally north. At 110th Street he turned sharply to the left, and very quickly we found ourselves traversing the northern edge of Central Park, with its low brick wall on our left. At Riverside Drive—almost at the western edge of the island—Sanderson turned right, resuming his northward course. I now had an instinct where he was heading: the George Washington Bridge leading to New Jersey, only opened two years before.

We crossed the bridge without incident. Once again the unreality of the whole enterprise began to overwhelm me. What exactly were we doing in this sedate car chase? I could easily have overtaken him, perhaps even cornered him on the street, the bridge, or the highway on which we were now cruising due west; but did I want to do that? What would I have done then? Shoot him in cold blood? Take him back to his Removal Company office? What then? Suddenly the incredible difficulty of resolving this whole matter struck me like a hurricane blast. I really had no idea why I was chasing Sanderson or what I was going to do if and when I caught him.

The mechanical effect of driving the car and shadowing Sanderson also freed up my mind to reflect on other things. Once again I was bothered by both the character of Sanderson himself—with his stilted diction, which sounded so phony—and by the completely bizarre nature of his Removal Company. Oh, the idea of "assisting" people in suicide wasn't so odd—could even have been considered admirable, in its way. It was the *utter cumbrousness* of his chosen method of giving people new personalities rather than actually dispatching them.

Sanderson may have been right in saying that this kind of switching of personalities may have been a bit easier than fabricating an entirely new personality, with all the documentation that might require; but the whole procedure was nevertheless incredibly awkward, time-consuming, and bothersome. What had he said? "It takes months, Mr. Scintilla, *months* to indoctrinate my 'victim,' as you term it, into his or her new personality." But the question remained: *Why would someone go to all that effort?*

Surely he could have devised some means of actually killing his victims and then disposing of the bodies. That was what his victims had wanted in the first place, and what their survivors had expected. Those survivors wouldn't be calling in the police, for in that case they really *would* be accessories before the fact. And the physical disposal of a body—especially for one of Sanderson's manifest medical skills—should not have been a great obstacle.

So we were back to the basic query: *Why? Why had Dr. Sanderson chosen this way to operate?*

I was not confident of ever answering that question.

We had been driving—rapidly, but not noticeably so—along Route 4 for some time, passing through the wealthy communities of Fort Lee and Englewood. Shortly after we crossed Teaneck Road, however, Sanderson suddenly veered off into a narrow country road whose name I didn't catch. What exactly was he doing now? Was this the moment that he would try to give me the slip? The chances of doing so were extremely remote: there were scarcely any turnoffs here except the driveways of farmhouses.

It was one of those early spring days when the transition from day to night comes with jolting suddenness. Uncannily, both Sanderson and I switched on our headlights at about the same time. There was practically no other traffic on this little-used road, and the beams from my car were fastened on his vehicle like a spotlight.

Once again, without warning Sanderson now turned off the road into a field of coarse, dry grass. The abruptness of the move had jounced his car up and down, and with my headlights I actually saw his head hit his steering wheel hard. That seemed to stun him for several moments, for his car weaved erratically, tearing up the grass and dirt of the unused field.

Sanderson stopped his car in the middle of the field. There was no one about. Only one dim farmhouse was visible, miles in the distance. It was now almost entirely dark.

I drew my car up about twenty feet away from his, my headlights still pinning it with light. I waited for his next move.

Sanderson got out of the car. His forehead was red with a bloody gash. He looked haggard, exhausted, and fearful. I could hardly comprehend the transition from the calm, self-possessed cynic who had had me in his clutches only a few days before.

There was a gun in his hand.

I got out of the passenger side of my car, so that my vehicle stood between my body and his. Pulling out my own gun, I trained it on him and said:

"Put it down, Sanderson. This is it! It's the finish!"

He didn't move. The gun wasn't even pointing in my direction, but instead was hanging down at the ground. I thought I saw his jaw trembling.

"Drop it, Sanderson!" I shouted. "You're done for!"

Almost instantly he shrieked at me, with more than a touch of madness in his voice: *"Kill me, you fool! What are you waiting for! Shoot me!"*

I paused, looking at him queerly. "I don't shoot a man in cold blood, Sanderson. Just give up and we'll go back to town."

Another shriek: *"No!"* Then Sanderson flung the gun away from him and sat down hard on the ground, leaning his back against his car. He covered his face with his hands.

I approached him carefully. The gun was about three or four feet away; he could easily have lunged for it if so inclined. I reached the gun and kicked it a little farther away.

"What's gotten into you, Sanderson?" I said, quietly. "What gives?"

He took his hands away from his face and looked up at me. He was the picture of wretchedness, the blood from his cut forehead trailing down one side of his head and almost dripping into his eye. His mouth was twisted into a grimace.

"You have me now, Mr. Joseph Scintilla," he said bitterly. "So why not just put an end to it? That's what you want, isn't it?"

"I'm not sure what I want," I said.

"You don't mean you intend to take me back *alive!*" he cried. The prospect seemed to appall him.

"Maybe," I said.

With a hideous scream he clutched the sides of his head with his hands and fell over on his side.

Infuriated, I grabbed him by the lapel of his coat and dragged him up. My face was inches from his. I hissed: "What's with you, Sanderson? What are you trying to pull?"

At that, he revived a bit—pushed me away from him with surprising vigor.

"Haven't you figured it out, yet, Mr. Detective?" he spat at me. "You're so good at finding people, but you don't seem so hot at understanding them...." His pedantic, schoolroom manner of speaking was entirely sloughed off: the real Sanderson, stripped of his cocoon of unnatural calmness, was laid bare before me.

When I made no reply, Sanderson looked at me with a kind of wonder, even of awe. "You really don't get it, do you? You just don't get the score!" He laughed harshly, hysterically. "I've led you here by the nose, and I can't get you to finish the job! Oh, it's too much!"

He howled with laughter.

"Come off it, Sanderson," I snapped. "What don't I get?"

"God, Scintilla, you're such a fool!" He looked right up at me. "Don't you see what I want? I know this is the end, I know you've destroyed my operation. There's nothing left for me—*so why can't you put me out of my misery?*"

I was brought up short. "You want me to kill you?" I said quietly.

"Yes!" he screamed. *"Yes!* That's all I want—nothing more!"

"Why?" I said.

"Why?" he repeated. His voice descended to a whisper. "Because it is *I*"—he pounded his own chest—"*I* who find the prospect of death so terrifying. The blackness, the oblivion, the utter extinction of life.... The very thought of it makes me feel as if I'm floating in some shoreless sea, helpless and deserted.... *Don't you see that's why I formed the Removal Company?*"

I looked at him quizzically.

"Do you think I wanted to kill anyone? The thought was too horrifying even to contemplate. And when I saw all these people—who really had so much to live for!—wanting to end their lives, I...I had to do something! This was the only way...fake their deaths and make them into new people. What else could I have possibly done? Yes, it was difficult, but it's all I could think of to help them.... I wanted to help them, really...."

He looked up at me pleadingly.

"You took their money, too."

"Oh, God, Scintilla, do you really think that was it?" he said scornfully. "Do you take me for a petty thief? Give me more respect than that."

He looked down at himself, scowling in furious contemplation. Then: "So why can't you finish me, Scintilla? It would be so easy for you...."

"I can't, Sanderson. I don't do things like that."

"Then what's going to happen to me?" he cried, pitiably.

"You know there's only one way."

"Wh-what?" he stammered, in genuine confusion.

I went over to his gun, lying in the grass and dirt.

I kicked it back at him. It hit him in the leg. He recoiled as if electrocuted.

"No...," he whispered. "No, please, not that...."

"Yes. It has to be that way. You started this, you have to finish it."

He picked up the gun, gazing at it in horrified fascination as if it were some alien entity whose nature and function he couldn't grasp. It rested in both hands for minutes.

"Go on," I said. "Take control of your life. Remember your own words. 'Suicide is never cowardly, it is always brave.' You were right.

"Be brave now."

His right hand wrapped itself around the barrel of the gun. His index finger momentarily touched the trigger, veered off, then resumed its hold. His hand, his whole body, began to shake. He looked up at me with an appalled expression.

"I can't...," he muttered. "I won't...."

"You will," I said, trying to instill in him the resolution I myself was far from feeling.

He looked down at the gun again. His face crumpled in horror.

"I tried to help people, Scintilla," he moaned. "I tried...."

"I know," I said. "But you ended up causing irreparable, inconceivable harm. Now you must put an end to it."

There was silence for several moments. Then, with a shriek, he held the gun to his temple and pulled the trigger.

CHAPTER TWENTY-FIVE

This was not a case whose loose ends were neatly tied.

By the time I got back to the Removal Company, I found that Vance and Merriwether had come upon an immense array of files that Sanderson had amassed, and had immediately shoveled them into a fire they had started in the fireplace of that paneled room where we had found Marge. Marge herself had come around, but was still groggy and weak-kneed. We let her rest while we continued to destroy the records.

As for Bullet Head—incredible as it may seem, we let him go. He was in no mood to stick around, and with his boss out of the way, he would surely be happy to see the back of this place. Frankly, we doubted that he would be telling anything to the police.

We had to call in the police ourselves, to deal with those two or three poor wretches whom Sanderson had been working on. I had called the precinct and had urged my pal, Lieutenant Monahan, to come along. Even my long friendship with him wasn't quite enough to make the explanations smooth or convincing: all I could say was that we had come upon a doctor conducting some kind of hypnotic experiments on people, and that didn't seem to satisfy Monahan in the least. But neither Arthur nor Gene nor I would say much more, and with a glare and a huff Monahan had to make do.

I have no idea what ever happened to those partially brainwashed people in the Removal Company.

* * * * * * *

Later we went back to 144 West 62nd Street to see how Katharine

Vance was doing.

Dr. Williamson was there. He gave me and my two male partners sharp looks over the smell of burning that covered us, and a still sharper look at Marge, still woozy from whatever drug Sanderson had administered. We did our best to prevent him from examining her.

I tried to deflect his attention by saying: "How is she, doc? What's the outlook for her?"

He glared at me for a time, still suspicious. He knew something had happened, couldn't figure out what it was, and sensed that we would never tell him.

"It's going to be a long haul, Mr. Scintilla," he finally said. "She has gone through an incredible trauma. I don't dare give her any drugs beyond the sedative, and even that I will give up soon. She needs to resume her life, and if she has the strength of mind and body to do it, then perhaps she will eventually recover."

I pulled him away from the others. "Doc," I whispered, "do you know of her...er, depression? How do we know that it won't...you know, come back even if she does 'recover'?"

"Yes, I know something about that," he said, "and I don't know what to tell you. I understand she had psycho-analysis, and it didn't appear to be of much help."

"Yes, well," I stammered, "perhaps some other doctor might be better for her...."

"Perhaps."

"When do you think she can go back to California?" I said more loudly, including the others in the conversation.

"A week, maybe a bit more. You know," the doctor ruminated, "a nice, comfortable train ride might be just the thing—"

"No!" shouted Vance. "Not a train ride! Not that!"

Dr. Williamson looked at him in quiet astonishment. We others looked away.

"As you prefer," Williamson said.

* * * * * * *

I spoke to Harry Greenway and prevailed upon him to have his marriage with "Elena Cavalieri" quietly annulled. We both realized that that would be far better than a messy, and public, trial for bigamy. I also spoke to Detective Gulliver Crane in Pasadena, explaining the situation—some of it—and persuading him that it would be in his best interest to drop the charges against Arthur Vance. He did so.

The murder of Dr. William Grabhorn was never solved.

* * * * * * *

A week passed. Vance and his wife were ready to go home. The two of them came to my office to say goodbye.

Vance placed his wife in a chair—she still seemed somewhat fragile and disoriented—then approached me as I sat on the edge of my desk. He shuffled his feet a bit in front of my desk, then said:

"Joe, I don't even know how to begin thanking—"

"Please," I said, holding up my hand. "Don't thank me. I just did my job. And I was paid well."

"Not well enough," Vance said gruffly, and he flung another stack of bills on my desk.

"Vance," I said, "you don't have to do this...."

"Yes, I do!" he replied excitedly. "You put your life on the line for me!"

"You did the same for me."

"Please, Joe, just take it—I'll feel better. You don't have to tell me that money doesn't solve every problem in the world, but it can help sometimes."

"All right," I conceded. "Thanks. Thanks very much."

Katharine Vance now approached me, timidly. "I don't know everything that has happened to me, but I know—Arthur has told me—that you are the person most responsible for...for saving me. I owe you my life," she said simply, hanging her head.

"Just make sure you take care of it," I said, giving her what I hoped was an avuncular hug.

We said goodbyes and they left.

Marge Schaeffer walked in a few minutes after they had gone.

"I wanted to see them up here," she said a little breathlessly, "but I met them in the hall—I guess they came up already. Are they going back home now?"

"Yes," I said.

"They're a nice couple," she said reflectively. "I wish them well."

"So do I."

We both stood still, not looking directly at each other.

"So what now, Joe?" she asked.

I shrugged. "I take on the next job, assuming there is one. Or"—looking at the big stack of money on my desk—"maybe I'll take a little vacation. It's been a long time since I've had one."

She looked right at me and said: "Feel like some company?"

I looked back at her and said: "That might be fine."

We stood grinning at each other. I felt like a kid.

"Say, Joe, do you like playing pool?"

"Do I—what?"

"Pool. You know, cue ball, sticks, table. You've heard of it, haven't you?"

I looked her up and down. "Gee, Marge, you don't look like the kind of gal who hangs out in a pool hall."

With a twisted smile she said: "Oh, there're plenty of things you don't know about me, Joe Scintilla."

There was nothing I could say to that.

"C'mon," she said banteringly, "let's play some pool."

"Okay," I laughed. "So long as you don't put me behind the eight-ball."

POSTSCRIPT

This novel was very loosely based upon a short story, "The Removal Company," by the Californian writer W. C. Morrow (1854-1923), published in the *California Illustrated Magazine* (October 1891) and not otherwise reprinted, to my knowledge. Morrow is a much undervalued writer of tales of suspense, horror, and the supernatural, and his work deserves to be better known. When I first read his story, I found it full of suggestive possibilities that could only be conveyed in a novel rather than a short story; moreover, his working out of the plot seemed a little tame by present-day standards. In the event that readers would like to compare my novel to its inspirational source, I print the complete text of the story below:

THE REMOVAL COMPANY

by W. C. Morrow

It is hardly strange that my best and oldest friend, widowed and dying, should have given into my charge her little daughter, Annette, for there was none other so strongly bound to this obligation, none toward whom that gratitude which lives beyond the grave extended a hand of gentler appealing. Nor did it seem at that time so serious an undertaking. Annette was sweet and gentle and quiet and obedient, studying my wishes and trying to follow their course, seemingly putting aside her own great sorrow in my presence and investing her demeanor with the full strength of her brave young heart. I knew little about children then, or I should not have been blind to the womanly conduct of this strange child. Now I have some idea of her suffering, which she kept so bravely from me, of that consuming yearning with all her childish heart for the touch of a mother's hand and the music of a mother's voice; and I know now how greatly she needed the kindly guidance of a level purpose and an even heart.

I thought I was doing the best I could. I imagined that the responsibility of the charge found proper estimation in my plans, in my conduct, and in my wishes. If there was a sense of oppression under it my gratitude would have masked it. So, being too young and unsettled to establish a household with Annette as my family, I put her in a convent. It never occurred to me to imagine that this sharp separation contained any element of a riddance, nor did there come up any formal hope that Annette, so desolate and lonely, so gentle, unselfish and retiring, might choose to become a conventual, upon which consummation my responsibility would cease, of course. When I spoke to her of going to school in a convent her sad face brightened, and then instantly it fell.

"What is it, Annette?" I asked.

"I can never see you then."

"Oh, yes," I said, "for I shall go to see you every week."

She looked up at me quickly. "You will come *every* week?" she asked.

"Yes; every week."

"Because," she added—but why did she use that word "because"? of what was it an explanation and for what a reason?—"because," she said in her sweet, low, childish voice, slightly tremulous, "you are all I have in the world."

I caught her up in my arms and kissed her for that, and this surprised her very much, for it was the first time I had ever caressed her, but that was because I knew so little about children. She went to the convent, and the years of her life began their steady course—with what loneliness, with what suffering, with what longings, with what numberless little cares and anxieties, with what small pleasures and diversions I did not know, for Annette was reticent, and it never occurred to me to inquire. My promise of visits suffered many violations, but my brave little girl never complained. There was always the same quick but transitory happiness which lighted up her pretty face when I would visit her; but there was otherwise a habitual sadness, growing deeper and surely merging into melancholy. And to my surprise she refused religious comforting—not that I was religious, but—I really did not know why her refusal troubled me. At times she talked sparingly but fearlessly a philosophy which made the good women there despair; these things they told me with concern.

The time came when I awaited with anxiety the day of her graduation, now close at hand, for responsibility at last had laid a hand upon me; its effect upon an erratic bachelor, not old enough to be Annette's father, was disquieting. Was there any element of selfishness in this feeling? Had I been a churl in failing often to visit Annette?—for when I did go I always took her some little present, and she was grateful for it. Could I not have gone oftener and taken her more presents? Could I not have stayed longer and been gentler and kinder to her, and told her things of the outside world to cheer her? Thus ran my thoughts, quickened possibly by conscience, as I sat in the very rear of the great room on graduation day, well concealed, I thought, by the large crowd present. Thus ran my mind as I sat and gazed in wonder at my Annette (for was she not my ward?) as she sat upon the platform with other girls. Could this beautiful girl be Annette? It must be, for she was so small, so fragile, so pale, so invested with an atmosphere of loneliness. In all that great room filled with people I saw only my little Annette; and never had I seen so pretty, so dainty, so exquisite a picture. I was glad she did not see me; I would let her know afterward that I had been there, and this would prove that I had not neglected her. She held the flowers which fortunately I had thought to send her, and her manner showed that by some accident I must have sent the kind she liked best; for in very truth I had ransacked San Francisco before I found any that I thought were good enough for Annette. But what meant this new look of trouble in her face? It appeared to be evidence of a tangible pain. A fear that the excitement had proved too great for her possessed me, and a strong pity was aroused. There was a strained expression in her eyes, whose glance wandered unceasingly over the vast audience, up and down, row by row, face by face, until the radiance from their unfathomable blue depths fell full upon me; and then instantly a bright flash of recognition, followed by a soft pink flush which rivaled the dainty coloring of her roses, swept over her face, and then a faint smile of pride and happiness, and her glance fell to the floor. At that moment there burst upon me unaccountably, with so fierce assailing that it stunned, the realization, all unexpected, all unguarded against, that my little Annette was a woman.

It was some days before I could recover full possession of myself, for by some unexplained means I had been thrown into a condition of wilder disorder than was customary even with me. Vaguely was Annette associated with this condition, and with a certain impatience I felt a resentment toward her—toward innocent, unhappy, unselfish Annette; and it added somewhat to my resentment to reflect that she was now eighteen, and beyond the legal reach of my protecting guardianship. It is true, she had no means for her maintenance, but I should not grudge her that from my modest earnings. This charge upon my income doubtless would keep me from marrying and having a home with all its sweet comforts, but was Annette to blame for that? and did this weaken the force of my obligation? And then, she might marry or become self-sustaining—. But at that moment the following note was brought to me:

> "My Dear Guardian:
> "You have not been to see me since the day of my graduation, but I am glad to know that you have not been ill. Perhaps it is better that you did not come, for I know that I should not have had the courage to thank you for all that you have done for me. How can I thank you now? Every word, look, and act of kindness from you through all these past years will remain a precious recollection.
> "Pardon me, my friend; but I can live no longer upon your bounty. I am a woman and of legal age, and my first right and duty are to maintain myself. Knowing your generosity and unselfishness, I must not let you know whither I go, but if all goes well with me you

shall know.

"Farewell, my best, my dearest friend.
Annette."

The blow was swift and cruel, but above all other feelings there struggled to the front one of bitter chagrin. So Annette had run away from me; so, after all, it was proved that I was nothing to her, and that now, when she was armed to make her own fight for life, she had no further use for me; so, she believed that my friendship was worthless, my guidance and assistance useless; and thus Annette had shaken me off as an ugly dream, leaving me bruised, humiliated, cut to the heart.

As the days passed by my resentment softened, and then there came upon me a fear that Annette's mind was deranged. Sometimes long ago I feared it, but not expected it. If I should find her with her mind awry, my duty would be clear; but if it should be otherwise how could I thrust my presence and friendship upon her? Her conduct had been a sufficient hint. The weeks passed, and my fear for her safety grew steadily. It looked bad that not a word had come from her. San Francisco was hardly large enough to afford absolute concealment, but it was large enough to starve in. How could Annette, with her dainty tastes, shrinking disposition and fragile body earn a livelihood there? Would she rather starve than be near me?

My fears finally impelled me to make a search, and for this purpose I employed a man named Greatwood. "I do not wish to see her," I instructed him, "nor does she wish to see me. If you find her tell her nothing, but report to me."

It was a harder task than I had imagined, but one day Greatwood came to me with a strange expression on his face. "I have found her," he said, "and she is in a very bad situation."

"Tell me about it, Greatwood," I begged, for his words gave me a quick, measurable pain and a great eagerness.

"Well," he said, "she has been sewing and trying to teach, but she was not strong enough, and her health broke down. It is a wonder she has lived so long. The people in the house have been kind to her, but she refuses to accept food from them, protesting that she is not in need of it. Matters reached a climax only last night. Some one heard a strange noise in the room—a very slight sound, but sufficient to attract the attention of a nervous woman in an adjoining room. She roused her husband, and they went to the girl's room. The door was locked; there was no answer to their calls and rapping. They burst open the door—"

"Is she still alive, Greatwood?" I gasped, springing to my feet.

"Yes; but they found something worse than her attempt."

"What was it, man?"

"She was starving."

"Come, Greatwood," I cried, "take me to her."

"But you said—"

"Come—there is not a moment to lose."

We went as fast as horses driven furiously could take us. Oh, what a shabby, wretched place for Annette, and the poor, bare room in which she lived! I went straight to the bedside and gently raised the slight, emaciated form of my poor Annette—*my* Annette, I say—and pressed her to my heart. She knew me, and feebly put her arms around my neck—the first time she had done this in all her life.

"I didn't think you would care to see me," she faintly said, and tears of happiness streamed down her wan cheeks; and there came into her beautiful blue eyes just such a look as that which lighted them up on the day when she found me in the great crowd at the convent. The doctor who had been summoned that night to attend her had left an injunction that she be given a broth; but the woman there told me that she had refused to take it. I ordered another at once. Annette watched me all the time, but said nothing, and her tears continued to flow. I was sure that I tried very hard to be kind and gentle with her. I said little, because she was very weak. I gave issue to not a word of chiding—how could I? But for all that there must have been something in my manner that disturbed her, for she soon became restless. What was there lacking in my conduct? Was it sympathy? Surely I felt it with all my heart. It is true, I could not forget Annette's past treatment of me—not that it should affect either my sympathy or my sense of duty, but that it indicated her dislike of my care and attention. I felt that I was guilty of a rude intrusion upon her now; for I was interfering in a manner that lay wholly between her and her Maker; and I found in her desolate condition a sufficient explanation of the fleeting happiness which she felt upon seeing me. This had worn off quickly enough, but not sooner than I had expected. Even before the broth arrived my presence had apparently become a positive annoyance to her. She shook her head, and I pleaded earnestly with her. Her look hardened all the more.

"But you must, Annette," I said.

Her eyes flashed with a quick look of defiance.

"No—come closer. Send the others away; I want to tell you something.... You are and always have been very kind to me...much kinder than I deserve or have ever deserved.... I can never repay you, because...I shall not live long enough."

"Annette!"

Her eyes brightened and a flush came into her deathly pale cheeks.

"It is true," she said, speaking more rapidly—"it is true. I am determined to go."

"What do you mean, Annette?"

"You know what I mean," she gasped, struggling to raise herself upon her elbow. "You know what I mean."

I knew then, for even if her words had failed to convey her dreadful meaning, the resolution in her beautiful eyes would have been sufficient information.

"You know what I mean," she repeated, "and it will be worse than cruel in you to interfere."

In spite of my philosophy; in spite of my belief in those unhappy days that the right to take one's own life was inherent, sacred, and inalienable; in spite of my conviction that none had the right to interfere and that all would better be dead than living; in spite of my opinion that among all those whom I knew—the sore afflicted, the deranged, the unhappy, the abandoned and desolate—none would find a happier release in death than my poor Annette,—in spite of all these things my heart seemed to die within me when a full realization of her terrible determination broke upon me. For my conscience was alarmed, and the memory of neglected visits and other attentions and kindnesses was aroused into unhappy activity. Possibly I could have made her life brighter and kept at bay the gloom and sense of loneliness that had become despair.

But what could be done? I knew that Annette was proud, and that the end of all things with her had come. Despite her generous effort to show appreciation of the little I had done for her so meanly, I saw that my presence was irksome and my influence an evil. What could I do?

"Annette, do you not think it is wrong to do what you contemplate?"

"Ah, yes," she replied, sinking back upon her pillow and covering her face with her hands.

"Then," said I, "you know you should not do it. I don't wish to dictate to you or preach a sermon, but let me assure you, Annette, that violence to conscience is unnatural and unholy, and that it is unworthy of you. Think well, my child.... And if I do not seem indelicate—how can I say without wounding you, Annette, that you need not fear the lack of such friendship in substantial form as I am able to give you?"

There was a long silence, and I knew that she was sobbing. Hope quickened within me, only to be strangled at once, for Annette brokenly said this:

"I appreciate your kindness and thank you with all my heart, but—but—I am determined."

Should I resort to harsh measures to restrain her? That would be mean and cowardly.... Annette must go.... That deadening realization forced itself upon me.... I would not interfere with the exercise of a right which I considered sacred.... Only one thing was left for me to do—I must be a friend now.

"Annette," said I, "if you have the strength to listen to me I will tell you something very strange, and suitable only for the ears of those who contemplate the end with the willing mind of one anxious to accomplish it. It will not save you to me, but it will save your conscience to you, and your wish will be gratified without outrage to your sense of right."

Annette fixed a very earnest look upon me.

"I don't understand how that can be," she said.

"You are too weak. Take some of this broth, and then I will tell you a thing exceedingly strange and of the deepest interest to you."

With surprising confidence in me, she swallowed the broth, and its good effect soon became manifest; and when a little color had come to her cheeks and a healthier brightness to her eyes, I told her substantially the following:

"I have a friend named Reiferth, a German of about my own age, and he and I have the same ideas concerning the matter that is in your mind. Now, as a fear of punishment in a future life deters many from committing the act who would be better off if not so restrained, Reiferth conceived the idea of forming a company which would undertake, for an ample consideration, to remove from this life, without inflicting pain, those who earnestly wish to go but fear to take the step for one reason or another, and who will submit themselves to the company to do for them what they fear to do for themselves. I refused, much to Reiferth's surprise, to become a member of the company; whereupon he charged me with inconsistency, and maintained that the purpose of the company was wholly noble and humane. I believed that it was, but I did not desire to embark in such an enterprise. Reiferth then declared that, knowing the scheme to be unlawful and its practice attended with the gravest dangers, with the penitentiary or the scaffold a constant menace to its success, I was afraid to become his associate. I made no rejoinder to that charge. Then Reiferth asked me to help him if it should come in my way, and I promised that I would. Reiferth put his plan in operation in the very heart of San Francisco, and there is evidence that he has prospered amazingly.

"Annette," I said in conclusion, "I offer you this opportunity for accomplishing your purpose without doing violence to your conscience. What do you think of it?"

[I have no desire to justify myself in this matter, nor to deny the right of criticism which the unusual position here advanced may invite; but while I know that the scheme here proposed may be denounced as but a form of suicide, and that its acceptance would bring all the penalties supposed to attach to that act, I have to say that I see little difference between its essence and that of knowingly acquiring habits and following practices which lead to the same result. It was important in this case that I impress upon Annette the idea of avoiding outrage to her conscience.]

Annette had listened with an interest that absorbed every faculty; and when I had finished she sat upright in great excitement, and somewhat to my dismay she said:

"Do you know where the place is?"

"Yes."

"What is it called?"

"The Removal Company."

"Will you take me to it?"

"Annette,—"

"Will you?"

"Immediately?"

"Yes; now."

"You are not strong enough, Annette."

"I am perfectly well," she responded, springing to her feet and commencing a few preparations.

With a heart so heavy that it almost dragged me to the floor I left the room and found my carriage still waiting. I went upstairs again, and Annette at once took my arm and walked firmly down to the street. So strange a numbness possessed me that I hardly believed I was in my right mind. In the carriage Annette, who was now all eagerness and activity, saw that something was wrong with me.

"Why," she cried, "you are ill!"

"I think not, Annette."

"I am taxing you too greatly—I am asking too much of you...but it will soon be over."

We arrived at the quarters of the Removal Company—a silent old brick house, with little exterior sign of occupancy. It was not far from the long warehouses that lie under the afternoon shadow of Telegraph Hill, and was in one of those districts which a vagrant fashion of migration had left a mere trace of former enterprise. Within the house all was brightness and modest luxury. Reiferth was a man of taste. He welcomed us very cheerfully. "I am sorry to see you ill, though," he said to me. He had a kind and gentle manner, and he handled with the utmost tact and delicacy the business in hand. I was hardly able to stand when Annette advanced to bid me farewell. Tears were in her eyes and she was pale, but her determination was firm and her courage unflinching. She took my hand and looked up into my face long and searchingly. What sought she there, if anything?

"Farewell, my friend," she said in a clear voice and with infinite tenderness.

"Annette,—"

But she stopped my words by throwing her arms around my neck, and before I could realize anything she had fled my presence, going with Reiferth to another part of the house. As soon as I could order my understanding I followed, but the door by which they had left was locked. No longer could I stand; an unaccountable weakness seized me, and I sank into the chair. There I sat an indefinite time in a stupor, and was thus sitting when Reiferth returned.

"Well?" I gasped.

"It is all over," he said kindly. Then he quickly brought me some brandy, which he made me drink.

"Where is she?" I asked.

"Upstairs."

"May I see her?"

"Why—no. I—I—don't think you ought."

"But I wish to."

After some further demur he yielded. He supported me up the stairs and into a room. On a lounge lay Annette. At the door my heart had bounded with gladness, for she appeared to be only sleeping; but when I had come nearer—I cannot write of all these terrible things even at this great distance of time. I had come to bid my poor Annette farewell now, for I could not, I could not in life.

"Please leave me, Reiferth," I begged.

When he was gone I took the slight body in my arms and pressed it close, very close to my heart. I covered the white, dead face with kisses. I kissed her hair, and her sightless eyes, once so beautiful, and caressed the poor sunken cheeks.

"Ah, Annette," I cried, "my own little Annette, *my* Annette, I can tell you now what I have learned this day—that I love you; that I love you with all my heart and soul, and have loved you thus since the day when you sought and found me in the great crowd at the convent. How blind and foolish I was, Annette! And now you are gone, and my heart is broken."

Reiferth came and took the poor dead body out of my arms and kindly led me away. My poor Annette!

* * * * * * *

More than a year had passed, and I was standing listlessly on a street corner in Philadelphia. I could not live in San Francisco, for everything there was eloquent with the memory of Annette. Darkness was approaching rapidly. I still stood, with that same dull pain which came upon me when Annette started down stairs with me to the carriage. The night was coming on cool wings, but its presence was soft and gentle. There was a shy touch on my elbow, and when I looked around I saw a beggar. She was small and slight, and was dressed in faded black. A black straw hat, with poor, cheap, faded lace, shaded her face from the street-lamp.

"Will you please give me a little money, sir?" she pleaded. "My husband has gone away, and I have nothing to eat, and my poor baby is starving."

It was not the voice alone that came to me out of infinite distance; there came crowding with it a thousand memories and all the anguish of a blasted life. I was a broken man, carrying existence heavily, but the eagerness which surged up within me swept aside all the torpor of my being. Some strange movement must have alarmed the woman, for she quickly raised her face...and there was not a trace of recognition in her eyes.

"Annette!" I cried. "You know me—your guardian—your old friend, who reared you from infancy—Annette!"

"I—I don't know you," she replied, with pitiful fright. "I am not Annette—I never had a guardian"; and honesty shone luminous in every word.

"But you *are* Annette," I protested, aghast, "and you must come with me."

"No, no!" she cried, with worse fright still; and then she turned and ran away.

I would not let her go so easily. I sprang forward and caught her, and held her firmly.

"Do you hate me so much as this, Annette?" I asked with angry and unreasoning bitterness. "Tell me so, and I will let you go."

"I don't hate you—I don't know you—you are mistaken. Let me go. I am afraid of you. I will cry out, and you shall be arrested."

I released her, and she hurried away. Was there really some dreadful mistake? Was it possible not to be certain of that low, sweet voice, those beautiful eyes (now strangely dull), that look of indescribable sadness, that small frail form, those exquisite graces of pose and movement? But if it were she, how could she, so honest and innocent, so much a stranger to deceit, conceal her surprise upon encountering me, and how assume entire ignorance of me? Here was a strange mystery—or—had I gone mad and taken to finding Annette in shadows? I glanced after her, and in the distance saw her hurrying along, fear lending fleetness to her step. Had I forgotten that Annette was dead?—but would not even her spirit know me? Without a thought of what I did I hurried after the flying form, which distance and darkness were absorbing—I would not lose Annette again. I went forthwith in pursuit, holding my pace within the necessities of its mission, getting a firmer hand upon my eagerness, and looking to the ordering of my purpose; for if ever a man needed to be bold yet cautious, firm yet gentle, fearless in strange, dark perils and reliant upon the evidence of his senses, that man was I. Enough had come forth already to distract my faculties; but Annette, dead or alive, had stood before me, and I would follow her now whithersoever the love which had bound me to her might lead.

Without once having looked back, Annette arrived in a dark street, slipped quickly into a door, and in a moment a tall, ugly house had swallowed her up. I was now close behind her. I tried the door. She had bolted it. I rushed upon it madly, burst it open, and sent it flying against the wall with a crash that resounded throughout the depths of the house; and as I did so I saw Annette—for I must call her so—clearing the top step. She turned and saw me, and fled with a cry. Never bounded a deer with swifter leaps than mine. I was close upon her in a dimly lighted hall, when she flung open a door, cried "Mother!" in a choking fright, and as I pushed into the room threw herself into the arms of a strange, sinister woman, wrinkled and bent with age. There the poor girl, her face buried in the woman's shoulder, sobbed and gasped and trembled in a very agony of fear. In a moment a powerful man of middle age came hastily into the room behind me, and stepped to one side to see me better. Other men followed him—men with dull, vacant faces, whose blankness would have impressed me at another time; but through all these faces and circumstances, through the turbulence of my emotions and the fierce energy of my purpose, there arose and stood forth the fact that this strong man and I were enemies—that between us two lay the settlement of this affair, and a dark pit yawned for him who should fall. He was the old woman's son; thus spoke his sharp eyes, somewhat dulled with drink, and his high cheek bones, like hers; the pose of his head and certain tokens of manner—all a copy of his mother's; but where coarse and brutal in him, sharp and cruel in her. Upon his body he wore only a woolen shirt, open at the breast, the sleeves rolled up, and upon his lower limbs coarse trousers.

"Well," said the man, his voice deep and his manner menacing, though betraying a puzzled mind, "who are you an' what yer tryin' to skeer them women to death fer?"

Annette, controlling a sob, raised her face upon hearing his voice, and looked at him gratefully.

"Joe," she said faintly, "I'm so glad you are here. You won't let him hurt me, will you, Joe?"

"Not as long as them hands kin close up a windpipe," responded the man, making a significant prehensile movement with his fingers; "but I don't think anybody wants to hurt yer, Bess. Now go to the baby."

Annette started and her lips opened. With a little cry she ran to a cradle in the corner—a very poor and shabby cradle—and tenderly lifted a sleeping infant. "Poor little angel," she crooned. "Did you think your mother had forgotten you?"

Its mother?

"Whose child is that?" I asked the man, and he noted the threat and challenge in my voice.

"I don't know what right you have—"

"I have a right, and we will not discuss it," I peremptorily interrupted.

"—to come here an' raise this rumpus an' skeer a couple o'

women, but if you'll be decent an' kind, like, about it, you kin ax my sister herself."

"Who is your sister?"

"Bess, there." He motioned toward Annette—Annette, gentle, dainty, refined, full of the softest graces—Annette the sister of this ruffian! "Come, Bess," said he, "brace up an' answer this man's questions. I won't let him hurt yer. You're jest as safe as you ever wuz in yer life. Tell him what he wants ter know, and tell it straight up 'n' down."

Thus encouraged—and, I could see, half commanded also—Annette (for I must call her that yet) turned and looked at me for the first time since I had entered the room. All hope that she might recognize me in the stronger light was dissipated instantly; she regarded me only with fear and uneasiness. I approached her closer.

"Annette," I said, removing my hat and looking down into her face as she sat holding the child—

"My name is not Annette," she hastily interjected.

"What is your name, then?"

"Elizabeth. My mother and my brother Joe call me Bess." This, looking up at me in the fullness of honesty, but perplexed and fearful.

"What is your other name?"

"Hartly. That is my husband's name."

I staggered under the blow, and the sharp eyes of the old woman and her son were fastened upon me with a steady gleam that burned.

"Whose child is that?" The words came with effort from a great depth within me.

"It is mine. Her name is Pearl. I am her mother."

Thereupon I went all astray from myself, and looked around with helpless dismay. The four sharp eyes were consuming me. Annette—may I so call her yet?—gazed steadily up at me with all her old gentleness and sweetness, but still with fear and anxiety. Beyond the four burning eyes were the faces of men who stared in blank stupidity. I looked down at Annette, and there too I saw now, not clearly, if at all, something of the stamp of vacuity which was upon the faces of these ragged men grouped near the door. I was groping in a gloomy path beset with deep pits, and I breathed uncertain dangers. The four eyes burned me with a glowing heat. In a tangle of betrayed senses I essayed a persistence which I hoped would drag Annette forth from what I conceived to be some grim and overmastering constraint.

"Where is your husband?" I asked.

Annette was puzzled or cautious, for her glance flew for help to the man Joe.

"Where is your husband?" I pressed it upon her, feeling that I possibly had touched a spring. The man's sharp gaze was transferred from me to her.

"Answer him fair, Bess," he said, not unkindly; "give him the straight truth."

"He has gone to sea," answered Annette, looking up at me in a wondering and troubled manner.

"When did he go?"

She appeared to be thinking very hard and sounding her memory for an honest answer.

"It was while I was ill," she finally said with some suddenness, and with much pride in her victory of recollection.

"You have been very ill?"

"Oh, yes; very ill indeed."

"When was it?"

"It was when my baby was born." (Here she began to speak with a quick, nervous energy.) "I didn't know it until a long time afterward—I was so very ill—and my husband was not with me. When I recovered I had forgotten I was married. I was in a strange—"

"Stop there, Bess," fiercely cried the man. She obeyed instantly and trembled. "You've got one o' them spells o' your'n agin, an' yer tellin' what yer don't know, an' yer lett'n yer tongue run away with yer senses. Forget yer husband! Forget yer was married! Maybe you've forgot I'm yer brother."

"No," faintly protested the girl, regarding him with wide eyes; "no, Joe; I haven't forgotten that, but I forget so many—"

"Who's this woman here?" demanded the man, indicating his mother.

"My mother. But, Joe—"

"Shup up! You've got one o' them crazy spells agin. Now, mister," added he, turning angrily upon me, "it's about time yer cleared out o' here, ain't it?" With increasing anger he continued: "You chased this here girl to her house, an' smashed in the door like a wild beast, and tore in here like as if you was goin' to murder the poor thing, an' now you've set her wits loose an' brung on another o' them wanderin' an' fergettin' spells. That's why I say you'd jist better clear out."

The man was in a rage; and, seeing that I did not move, he stepped to the chimney and took an axe-handle from the corner. At this juncture the old woman came out of her silence.

"No, Joe," she said with a strong, quiet firmness; "don't lose yer head, my son, for yer need a cool brain an' a stiddy nerve right here and right now. There's jist a misunderstandin' summers, an' it'll come out all right." Joe became quiet, and his mother turned to me and said: "You look lack a gentlemun, sir, an' no doubt you air; an' yer don't look lack you'd been a-drinkin'; but you'll allow you've acted very queer—I may say outrageous-like—an' my son ain't to be blamed fer gittin' mad at yer. Now, to save my blessed life I don't know what yer drivin' at, but I b'lieve yer actin' on good principles and have mistook this girl fer summon else, 'cause you've been callin' her Ninette, or somethin'. You suspec' there's somethin' wrong, an' yer think yer know the girl, an' want ter get her out o' this scrape." And so the woman talked on, reviewing the whole situation with uncommon skill, reminding me that the girl did not know me, that in all her answers she had tried to tell the truth so far as a shattered mind would permit. The woman closed a long speech by going into a tedious history of the girl's life and assuring me that unrestricted opportunity would be given for an official investigation on the morrow. But the whole of this fine effort passed without effect upon me.

"No!" I exclaimed. "I will not trust her another night in your devilish hands. There is some crime here of so damnable a character that it overwhelms your lies. I will spare you the law on condition that you stand aside and let me take away this girl in peace."

Upon saying that I picked up Annette and her child and advanced toward the door, but the fury of the man Joe escaped restraint, and he sprang before me with his weapon aloft.

"No!" he cried with an oath; "not while I'm alive."

In an instant I had put Annette aside and sent a chair flying through the glass window. I leaped to the opening it made and cried out with all my strength. The call for help went bounding up and down the street from other throats, and swift feet were set in motion. I glanced back upon my enemies. The furious ruffian, taken unaware, had stood a moment in a stupor; but now, having roused himself, he came upon me with the one purpose of killing me. At that moment the shrill whistle of a policeman, always a thing which strikes upon one's sensibilities much as a physical blow, went at large upon the night and thrilled all the ruffian's nerves and drew the sap from his purpose; pallor swept over his face, his hand dropped.

"Joe," called his mother, in sharp anxiety, "git them fellers away quick an' come back here. *We'll see yit.*"

The man, quickened by a sense of danger, hustled away the dumb blank creatures and returned simultaneously with two officers, who headed a procession of frightened and curious people.

"Shut the door," I called out. The officers came within and the door was closed upon the crowd.

"Who was it called for help? What is the matter?" asked one of the officers.

"It was I who called," I answered.

"Oho, Simpson!" said the same officer, addressing Joe. "Trying to do this man, eh? You've been quiet so long that I thought you had given up that sort of thing and was sticking to the begging business.... Well, what has he been trying on you, sir?" concluded the officer, addressing me.

"Nothing, I assure you," I replied, "but this girl, whom I have known from infancy—I found her here and would have taken her away, but this man tried to kill me. I want you to help me rescue her from this fearful den."

"That girl with the child? Oh, she's one of Simpson's best beggars!"

Upon his requesting it, I gave a relation of all that had happened since I first saw Annette on the street. "She is one of his beggars, you say," I added; "there is yet a deeper and more damnable infamy. They say she is married. It is a lie; but see, she is a mother!"

"Ah!" exclaimed the officer, fixing a hard look upon Simpson, who, encaged within grave suspicions, appealed with his eyes to his mother. She thereupon said:

"I'd lack ter speak a word private to this gentlemun."

I went with her into a corner of the room, and we whispered.

"What yer want ter do, sir?" she asked.

"I intend to take this girl to the police station."

"Ah, well! She's dementy, like; an', 'twixt you an' me, I ain't sorry ter git rid of her."

"You and your son also will go to the station, but as prisoners, to be tried and punished for your crimes."

This to her was not unexpected; but she fastened her gaze upon me with a penetrating, sinister, unwavering manner, and it hurt.

"I don't think you'd better do that," she said, not relaxing her gaze, and speaking very slowly. "Once there was a man what connivered in schemes fer to *remove* people what didn't have the sand fer to kill theirselves, an' when some folkses found it out they blowed on him, an' he spent the rest of his life in the state's prison.... Me 'n' my son don't want no trouble with *you*, an' you don't look lack a gentlemun what's got a wobbly tongue."

I left her and returned to the officers. Annette sat holding her child tenderly, but with a look so pathetic and helpless, so confused with fright and a shaken consciousness, that while I yearned to comfort her I could see that whatever little mind she had was drifting away. I said to the officers:

"I wish to take this girl and her child to Dr. Arnold's hospital. Will you kindly help me?"

"And Simpson goes to the station?" I heard the sharp clinking of handcuffs.

"No—not to-night; there is time for that. Help me in the present urgency."

Annette's resistance was slight, and there was no other. She sobbed all the way in the carriage, and talked incoherently to her fretting child. She was made comfortable in the hospital, but she sobbed continuously. "Her dementia," said Dr. Arnold, "is almost complete. The shock has been too great." I took him wholly into my confidence, omitting not even the Removal Company and Annette's experience there. He asked me many questions; his mind was quicker and deeper and shrewder than mine. "Without knowing it," he said, after a long silence spent in pacing the floor, "you have unearthed a singular and original form of crime. The Removal Company has never killed any one."

I looked at him amazed and incredulous.

"Not one," he continued. "The victims were simply treated with a drug which destroyed their minds partly and their memory wholly. Are you so confiding as to believe that Reiferth would have dared take any one's life? The risk was too great, and the plan lacked that merit of continued profit which distinguishes the one in actual operation."

I did not understand him.

"With wrecked minds the victims would make good beggars," explained the doctor. "The wretches are sent from San Francisco to Philadelphia, where the danger of recognition is small, and are kept as beggars under the reliable agency of Mr. Joe Simpson and his mother; and your Removal Company has a steady income through their zeal. The blank-faced men whom you saw at Simpson's, as well as this poor girl, have been subjected to the peculiar treatment of the Removal Company, and are employed as beggars."

I think I hardly understood all of this at the time, for I was weak from a great strain, and nervously awry from a certain strange, wild joy for having Annette alive and under my care once more.

"Can you restore her to her former condition of mind?" I asked.

Gravely and slowly he made answer: "There is a bare possibility.... The plan must be heroic and desperate.... If it fails—death or complete dementia."

It came out afterward, in an investigation of Simpson's methods, that my poor Annette, whose innocence and sweetness must have been her guard against even the lowest brutality, had never been a mother; that was a deception practiced upon her to make her captivity surer.

"Ah," exclaimed Annette, upon emerging, after many days, from those great depths, "I am still alive! Why did not Mr. Reiferth keep his promise? Have I been asleep long?"

Ay, more than a year, Annette; but the hideous dreams of that black and terrible time have left no stamp upon your memory!

* * * * * * *

The sweet, cool western wind and the generous sunshine come to California, bringing their blessings to the rich and the poor, the prosperous and the unfortunate, the happy and the despairing; but I think that the gentle winds and the shining years bless with a special grace one happy home, which, born of suffering, of strange misunderstandings, of crime, of darkness, has issued forth into the broad yellow light that heaven sends, grateful, humble, inexpressibly content. That home is ours—Annette's and mine; for not alone have the church and the law made us man and wife.

www.ingramcontent.com/pod-product-compliance
Lightning Source LLC
Chambersburg PA
CBHW022154260626
47155CB00018B/1870